An Icicle W9-CEQ-121

"Oh, thank you . . . thank you," Mavina said. "Now I need . . . not be . . . frightened . . . any-more."

"I shall be very offended if you are," the Major said. "And tomorrow I will ask someone on board to chaperon you until we reach Calcutta."

Mavina's eyes widened before she asked, "Is . . . that . . . necessary?"

"I am afraid that the gossips will think it is," the Major answered. "I have not introduced myself. I am Major Willoughby Wicke, attached to the Viceroy's staff, and therefore, as you can understand, I have to be careful of my reputation!"

He was smiling as he spoke, and Mavina gave a little laugh.

"In other words, you are . . . worrying about . . . mine."

A Camfield Novel of Love
by Barbara Cartland

———

Camfield Place,
Hatfield
Hertfordshire,
England

Dearest Reader,

Camfield Novels of Love mark a very exciting era of my books with Jove. They have already published nearly two hundred of my titles since they became my first publisher in America, and now all my original paperback romances in the future will be published exclusively by them.

As you already know, Camfield Place in Hertfordshire is my home, which originally existed in 1275, but was rebuilt in 1867 by the grandfather of Beatrix Potter.

It was here in this lovely house, with the best view in the county, that she wrote *The Tale of Peter Rabbit*. Mr. McGregor's garden is exactly as she described it. The door in the wall that the fat little rabbit could not squeeze underneath and the goldfish pool where the white cat sat twitching its tail are still there.

I had Camfield Place blessed when I came here in 1950 and was so happy with my husband until he died, and now with my children and grandchildren, that I know the atmosphere is filled with love and we have all been very lucky.

It is easy here to write of love and I know you will enjoy the Camfield Novels of Love. Their plots are definitely exciting and the covers very romantic. They come to you, like all my books, with love.

Bless you,

CAMFIELD NOVELS OF LOVE
by Barbara Cartland

A NEW CAMFIELD NOVEL OF LOVE BY

Barbara Cartland

An Icicle in India

JOVE BOOKS, NEW YORK

AN ICICLE IN INDIA

A Jove Book / published by arrangement with
the author

PRINTING HISTORY
Jove edition / December 1995

ISBN: 0-515-11770-6

A JOVE BOOK®
Jove Books are published by The Berkley Publishing Group,
200 Madison Avenue, New York, New York 10016.
JOVE and the "J" design are trademarks
belonging to Jove Publications, Inc.

PRINTED IN THE UNITED STATES OF AMERICA

10 9 8 7 6 5 4 3 2 1

Author's Note

As I have explained in this book, the members of the East India Company did not originally intend to govern India but merely to make money there.

They did this very effectively throughout the 18th century.

But when the British took over, they were determined to reform their subjects, especially with regard to the Thuggee.

The Thuggee, who worshipped the Goddess Kali, were a cruel but hereditary fraternity of stranglers who had for hundreds of years terrorised travellers in India.

They had their own hierarchy, traditions, and rituals.

They believed that when they strangled strangers on the road they were strangling in the cause of Kali for Kali herself.

The Thuggee had a great deal of secret protection from important Indians. Being a brilliantly organised secret, it was extremely difficult to combat them.

The man who picked up the challenge was Captain William Sleeman, who had gone to India in 1809.

He first became interested as a Magistrate and District Officer in central India in the ghastly mystery of the Thugs.

Patiently and methodically he learned all he could about the sect.

By 1820 it had become his prime interest in life to destroy them.

The Thugs worked in absolute secrecy, but they were highway murderers.

When they found a group of travellers upon the road, they would infiltrate themselves into their company with ingratiating talk and often join them on their journey for a day or two.

Then, when the moment and the place seemed suitable, and the omen auspicious, they would kill their companions with a well-tried technique of noose-work, knee, and grapple.

They strangled them from behind with the yellow noose known as a *rumal*.

In central India, Sleeman estimated that the odds against a citizen's safe passage were almost two to one.

It was reckoned that 40,000 people were killed by the Thugs each year.

Sleeman did his best, and by about 1833 Thuggism had diminished an enormous amount.

At the same time, no-one could keep complete track of every traveller who disappeared, and there were reports of Thuggee murders as late as 1904.

chapter one

1886

"*AND everything else, my house, money, and possessions I leave to my wife, Lucy, unconditionally.*"

The Solicitor's voice droned to an end.

The people sitting in front of him looked towards Mrs. Lonsdale.

Some were envious, some compassionate, and it was obvious that none of the other relations had been left anything.

Then, before anyone could speak, the Solicitor said:

"There is a codicil to the Will which was added six months ago."

Several people who had been rising from their seats sat down again.

He read:

"*To my Niece, Mavina Lonsdale, the sum of five hundred pounds, unconditionally.*"

This was a surprise and was followed by a buzz of voices.

Mavina felt she could not have heard right.

She had never imagined for a moment, when after the funeral they were told the Solicitor would read the Will, that her Uncle would leave her anything.

He had, she thought, always resented the fact that she had come to live with him when she had nowhere else to go.

She had always felt she was a charity child and must be grateful for the roof over her head.

When her Father had been killed in India, she found it impossible to accept that, for some reason no-one understood, all his money had vanished.

Apparently he had drawn it out of his Bank in England two months before he was killed.

No-one had any record of what had happened to it.

Colonel Richard Lonsdale was serving with his Regiment in India when he met his wife.

After a few years, he had been transferred to England at his own request and had continued his military service at home instead of abroad.

He was a little later transferred to a special Department in the War Office.

He had then bought an attractive house only a short distance outside London.

He managed to return home every evening to be with his wife and his small daughter, Mavina.

They were extremely happy until two years ago, when Mavina was sixteen, her Mother died one cold winter.

It happened so quickly and unexpectedly that it was difficult at first to realise the impact of it.

Colonel Richard Lonsdale soon found it impossible

to continue coming home every night to a house which did not contain the woman he loved.

Mavina then began to realise that everything had changed.

Almost before she was aware of what was happening, her Father had been transferred from the War Office back to India.

She was sent to a Finishing School which was exclusive and very expensive.

However, her Father promised her that as soon as her education was complete, she could join him in India.

"That will be wonderful, Papa," Mavina said. "I will work very hard and you will be proud of me."

"I am always proud of you, my Dearest," Colonel Lonsdale replied. "In fact, they have been asking me to return to my Regiment for some time, but I would not leave your Mother."

He read the question on his daughter's lips before she asked it, and added:

"Yes, I know I met her out there and she loved India as much as I do. But the Doctor said she was not strong enough to stand the excessive heat, so I brought her back and stayed here."

There was a bitterness in his voice as he added:

"Perhaps if we had gone back to India she would still be alive."

Because she knew how distressed her Father was, Mavina could only slip her hand into his and say:

"I love you, Papa, and I only hope that the months go by very quickly before I can join you."

When she learned that her Father was dead, she could hardly believe it.

How could he have died and left her?

When the formal notification of his death arrived,

she learned it was while he was "on active service."

She was quite sure, although the War Office did not give any details, that he must have been fighting on the North-West Frontier.

He had talked about it so often.

She almost felt as if she knew as much about India as if it were her own country.

But on her Father's death everything had changed.

Her Uncle told her, obviously reluctantly, that she could stay for one more term at the Finishing School.

Then she must come and live with him and her Aunt Lucy.

"What about our house?" she asked in a bewildered tone.

"You must face the fact," her Uncle said, "that your Father has left no money at all. There are quite a number of debts which will be paid off by the sale of the house. Then there will be nothing for you to live on, except, of course, that I will provide for you as best I can."

There was a grudging note in his voice which made Mavina want to say she would manage without his charity.

Then she knew it would be impossible.

She had been very well educated, thanks to her Father and Mother, and especially at the Finishing School, to which she had gone after her Mother's death.

But that did not equip her to earn her own living.

She thought perhaps she could be a governess.

But who would employ a girl of eighteen to look after their children?

'There must be something I can do,' she thought desperately, but she had no idea what it could be.

After packing her own clothes and her Mother's, she left her home.

She took with her only a few things which she had refused to allow to be sold.

"There is no room for any of the furniture in my house," her Aunt had said firmly.

Her Uncle had added:

"I know you prize the books in your Father's collection, but they, too, would take up too much room. I will allow you to keep twenty of them, the rest can be sold in their book-cases."

When she was alone at night, Mavina wept.

Her tears were not only for the loss of her Father and Mother, but because she herself was left alone and empty-handed.

Her Uncle's house in London was small and dark and definitely gloomy.

It looked out onto a narrow street.

Although the rooms were well furnished, they had none of the individual taste in their decoration which had made Mavina's home in the country unique.

People who came to it had exclaimed:

"How pretty your house is! There is an atmosphere of happiness about it we have never found anywhere else."

It was not only the atmosphere which was different, Mavina thought.

Her Father and Mother had brought back from India the most beautiful materials with which they had made the curtains and covers for the sofa and chairs.

They were the colours, Mavina knew, of saris.

They complemented the carvings and the other articles from India which stood on every table and hung on every wall.

She would never willingly have parted with them.

Having known them since she was a baby, she felt they were part of her life.

Without telling her what he was doing, her Uncle sold them to a Professor of Indian history.

He gave, she understood, quite a good price for everything that her Father and Mother had collected and loved.

"They were mine, Uncle! They were mine!" Mavina said angrily when she heard what had happened.

"The sum I received for them will help to pay your Father's debts," her Uncle said quietly.

He went on before she could speak.

"When the negotiations for the sale of the house are finished, I hope there will be no debts outstanding. But to put it frankly, my dear Niece, there will also be nothing over for you."

Mavina could not understand it.

When she learned her Father had drawn all his assets out of his Bank and had the money transferred to India, she found it even more incomprehensible.

"Surely there are people we can write to and find out what has happened," she said to her Uncle.

"I have told your Father's Solicitors to do that," he replied, "but you must be aware, Mavina, that they do not work for nothing. Quite frankly, I have spent enough time and money on your Father's Estate already."

There was nothing she could say.

She was aware every day that passed after she had moved into her Uncle's house that her Uncle was expecting her to be excessively grateful because he provided for her.

Now, when she learned that he had left her five hundred pounds, she could not believe it.

She wished he had told her he was doing so, so

that she could have thanked him.

Now it was too late.

As the relations in their black gowns and veils said goodbye, nearly every one of them murmured:

"Congratulations, Mavina. I am sure you are delighted that your Uncle thought of you."

Finally they had all gone.

Mrs. Lonsdale thanked the Solicitor for coming, and he hurried away as if he were glad the task was over.

The maid, without being told, brought in the tea.

It was rather too early for it, but she was sure that was what her mistress needed.

"Thank you, Emily," Mrs. Lonsdale said. "I am sure it will make me feel better."

"Now, don't go upsetting yerself, Ma'am," Emily, who had been with the family for years, said. "There's no arguing with th' Lord, and th' Lord has taken 'im to 'is rest."

Mrs. Lonsdale sat down on the sofa, wiping her eyes as she did so.

She had not cried at the funeral, which Mavina had thought was brave of her.

She was, in fact, a very undemonstrative woman.

Now, when Emily had left the room, she drank a little of the tea and said in a low voice:

"I shall miss Arthur. I think the best thing I could do would be to sell this house and go and live in the country with my Brother."

"If you think you would be happier there," Mavina replied, "that is a good idea."

"I know he will have me," her Aunt replied, "and I suppose he will take you too."

Mavina did not reply immediately, and after a moment her Aunt said:

"Now that your Uncle has left you all that money,

you can certainly pay for your food, if nothing else."

There was a note in her voice which told Mavina all too clearly that she resented her inheriting any money from her Uncle, certainly as much as five hundred pounds.

She had always known her Aunt was mean.

She cheese-pared in buying food and everything else which concerned the household.

Sheets had to be darned, until one of the servants said jokingly:

"They look like a tennis-net."

The boxes of matches were counted, and if a plum or an apple from the Dining-Room went missing, Mrs. Lonsdale was aware of it.

From the way she had spoken now, Mavina knew what would happen.

If she went to live with her Aunt's Brother, as she had suggested, the money she had been left would gradually be spent week by week.

Eventually there would be nothing left.

She put down her cup of tea from which she had taken only a few sips.

In a voice which sounded braver than she felt she said:

"It is very kind of you, Aunt Lucy, to suggest I should come with you to the country. But now that Uncle Arthur has been so generous, I have decided exactly what I shall do."

"What is that?" Mrs. Lonsdale asked sharply.

"I am going to India to find Papa's grave," Mavina replied.

If she had thrown a bomb in the middle of the room, she could not have caused more of a sensation.

Mrs. Lonsdale was horrified at the idea and said so in no uncertain terms.

The argument continued all through supper.

When Mavina went to bed she was even more determined than she had been earlier in the day that she would go to India.

She had been only a child when she came home with her Father and Mother.

Yet India was still as vivid in her mind as if it had been yesterday.

The beauty of the country, the colour, the sunshine, the smiling faces she remembered, were all something that was still in her dreams.

"I will go to India!" she told herself.

She felt that her Father was approving her decision.

"I cannot stay here, Papa," she said as if he were beside her, "and have nothing to do. I am quite sure that if Aunt Lucy takes me to the country, I shall be nothing but an extra hand in the house and not be paid for it."

She thought perhaps she could teach children in India.

Her Aunt had pointed out to her that she would have to wait years before anyone would engage her in England.

Anyway, for the moment she could pay her way.

She would be travelling across the country her Father had loved and served for so long, until she found where he was buried.

She expected it would be far up in the North.

Although her Uncle had said he had asked the War Office for details, they had not been forthcoming.

She went to sleep repeating "India, India" over and over again.

Not surprisingly, she dreamt she was back there and the sun was shining brilliantly.

She was happy with a happiness she had not known for a long time.

When morning came, Mavina learned that her Aunt had gone out early.

She took the opportunity to go out herself.

She knew, because she had seen her Father off when he returned to India after her Mother's death, that the ships sailed from Tilbury Docks.

She found her way to the booking-office of the Peninsular and Oriental Shipping Line in the City by a bus which went part of the way from Hyde Park Corner.

Then she had to change to another.

She had to wait until three or four people in front of her had been served.

Finally she was able to ask when the next Steamship would be leaving for India.

"The day after tomorrow," the Clerk behind the counter replied.

He spoke quite casually.

Then, when he looked at Mavina's pretty face, he said in a very different tone:

"Can I help you, Miss?"

"If the ship is not fully booked," Mavina said a little nervously, "I want to travel to Calcutta."

The Clerk looked at some papers and asked:

"First or second class, Miss?"

"Second, please," Mavina replied.

She thought it would be a mistake to spend too much of her money on the voyage from England.

She knew anyway it would be expensive.

She wanted to have plenty left to spend in India, especially if she was to get as far as the North-West Frontier.

She had no idea if that was even possible.

But she felt sure that if her Father had been killed there, that was where he would be buried.

"Do you mind an inside cabin, Miss?" the Clerk was saying. " 'Cos as I expects you know, it's not as expensive as them that are on the outside."

"I will take the cheaper one," Mavina said.

Her Father had opened an account for her and given her a cheque-book before he left for India.

She had brought her cheque-book with her.

"I have left enough money in your account," he had said, "for your education until the time you leave school. Also for the wages of the servants in the house and, of course, for what you will spend every month on food. If you want any more, you must write and tell me so. But I think you will find I have provided enough."

"I will be as economical as I can, Papa," Mavina promised.

"I want you to have everything you need within reason," her Father assured her. "Then, when you join me in India, we will have plenty of money with which to indulge ourselves."

Mavina had flung her arms round his neck and kissed him, but not because she was grateful for the money. It was because she loved him.

It was agony now that her Mother was dead, to be left alone in England.

"I shall pray, Papa," she said, "that the time will go very quickly and then I will be with you again."

"I shall be counting the days too," her Father answered. "I have a great deal to do in India at the moment, but when you come I want to show you some of the beauty of the country I love and which I am proud to defend."

The way he spoke the last words told Mavina he would be fighting.

"Be careful, Papa," she said. "Remember that I need and want you."

"I shall not forget that," Colonel Lonsdale replied. "And, my precious little daughter, work hard at school, as I have asked you to do, and when we are together again I will explain to you why it is so important."

Mavina had a vague idea of its importance already.

However, she did not say so, but only kissed her Father again.

She had stayed with him on board the P. & O. Liner until those who were not travelling were told to go ashore.

She had kissed him again, then stood on the quay, waving as the ship moved slowly out of the dock into the River.

Only when her Father was out of sight and she could no longer see the ship for her tears did Mavina turn away.

Her Father had arranged for her to stay the night with her Aunt and Uncle before she returned to school.

The Hackney carriage he had hired was waiting to take her there.

She cried for a little while in the carriage.

Then she told herself that as a soldier's daughter she must behave like one and the time would soon pass.

It had passed and she was waiting for a letter from her Father to say she could join him.

It was then that a War Office *communiqué* informed her Uncle with the deepest regret that Colonel Richard Lonsdale was dead.

At first Mavina found it impossible to believe.

Then, when she knew it was the truth, she cried until she was utterly exhausted.

How was it possible that she had lost both her Father and her Mother?

She was now alone in the world except for her Uncle and Aunt, whom she had never liked.

She was also convinced they did not like her.

Yet she had had to go and live with them, feeling as if she were entering a prison from which it would be impossible to escape.

Now her Uncle, of all people, had given her the key to freedom!

She was determined that nothing and no-one would stop her going to India.

She knew as she found her way back from the shipping-office that her Aunt would be angry.

She had deliberately taken matters into her own hands too quickly for them to be altered.

She expected her Aunt had already written to her brother to say she was bringing Mavina with her when she came to the country.

She had doubtless added her niece would be able to pay towards her keep.

Mavina was late for luncheon when she arrived back at the ugly, dark house she had hated from the first moment she saw it.

Her Aunt was waiting for her.

"Where have you been, Mavina?" she demanded. "I understand you left the house early this morning, and look at the time now!"

"I have been to the offices of the P. & O. Shipping Line," Mavina said.

Mrs. Lonsdale stiffened.

She did not speak, she merely looked hostile.

"I have booked a passage on the *Coromandel,* which is sailing for India the day after tomorrow."

"You have no right to do such a thing!" her Aunt said angrily. "I have already told you that I will take you to my Brother in the country."

"I am determined to go to India and find Papa's grave," Mavina said. "Thank you for thinking of me, but I feel sure your Brother will understand why I must refuse his hospitality."

"The whole idea is ridiculous," her Aunt expostulated. "The money your Uncle left you will support you for a long time if you are careful."

"It will also get me to India," Mavina said, "and I expect, once I am there, if my money runs out, I shall be able to find something to do, if it is only looking after small English children."

"Well, you have made your decision," Mrs. Lonsdale said, "and all I can say is I think you are an extremely stupid young woman to throw away good money which, I assure you, you will never have again."

"I also want to try to find out what has happened to Papa's money," Mavina said. "He drew it out of the Bank in England, and it must have been for a good reason."

She paused and then continued:

"Perhaps he invested it in some way and did not have time to tell me what he had done before he was killed."

"That is all speculation," her Aunt retorted. "As I have told you already, I am quite certain your Uncle meant you to keep that money and use it sensibly until you got married."

Mavina prevented herself from saying it would have been very difficult for her to find a husband.

While she had been living with her Aunt and Uncle, she never met any men.

She supposed it would be the same with her Aunt's Brother.

He lived in a very isolated part of the country, where he farmed.

Aloud she said:

"I hope I will get married one day, but in the meantime I want to find out about Papa, and, of course, to see India again."

"Well, you have made your bed and you must lie on it," Mrs Lonsdale snapped. "I only hope that you will not be disappointed."

The way she spoke told Mavina only too clearly that she was quite certain she would be.

However, there was no point in arguing.

Mavina went upstairs to start re-packing the things she had unpacked when she arrived.

It took her a long time because she now unpacked the clothes she had brought from home which had belonged to her Mother.

There were thick coats and furs amongst them.

These, Mavina thought, she would certainly not want in India.

She kept for herself one coat and a very pretty embroidered shawl which her Mother had sometimes worn in the evenings.

All her thin dresses fitted her almost perfectly.

She and her Mother had been the same size.

Mrs. Lonsdale was very beautiful, and her Father had often laughed and said they looked more like Sisters than Mother and daughter.

"If I were a stranger," he said, "I would not know which was the younger."

"But you would give Mama the prize for being the

more beautiful," Mavina remembered saying once.

"Of course," her Father had answered. "Your Mother is the most beautiful person I have ever seen. When I first saw her, I thought she could not be real and had just stepped out of my dreams."

His wife smiled at him.

Then, as if he felt he was neglecting Mavina, he said:

"One day, my precious daughter, you will be nearly as beautiful as your Mother."

"I hope so, I do hope so, Papa," Mavina answered.

Her Mother kissed her and said:

"Do not listen to your Father. You are very lovely now just as you are, and we are lucky to have such a very pretty daughter."

Mavina picked up one of her Mother's dresses and, holding it up in front of her, went to the mirror.

It was difficult to know if she was as pretty as her Mother.

She had the same fair hair.

"As golden as dawn," her Father had said once.

Her eyes were very large, and for some reason her eyelashes were dark.

"Blue eyes put in with dirty fingers, the Irish say," her Father had teased her.

Mavina also saw that her skin was very white, just like her Mother's.

Mrs. Lonsdale used to say:

"I never got sunburnt. It made the other English women in India furious, because even a touch of sun made them red or brown, while my skin remained white."

Mavina knew she could say the same.

She remembered her Father saying to her Mother:

"You have a skin like a magnolia. It was one of the

first things I noticed about you."

"The first thing I noticed about you," her Mother had replied, "was that you were the tallest and most handsome man I had ever seen."

Looking at herself in the mirror, Mavina thought she ought to be beautiful with two such good-looking parents.

She put her Mother's pretty dresses back into the trunk, then extracted two black ones Mrs. Lonsdale had worn at funerals.

"I do not like you in black," the Colonel had said on one occasion.

"I know, Darling," his wife had answered, "but I can hardly go to the Lord Lieutenant's funeral wearing a pretty colour."

Her Husband had kissed her.

"I love you whatever you wear," he said. "But most of all when you look like a white rose or when you are dressed up looking like an exotic orchid."

They had both laughed at this.

Mavina thought she too wanted someone who thought she looked like a flower.

The rather dull frock she was wearing at the moment did nothing for her.

'When I get to India I will wear Mama's clothes,' she told herself. 'But I think my own, which I had at school, will be more appropriate on board ship.'

The ship was not sailing until late in the afternoon.

However, there seemed to Mavina no point in hanging about the house with her Aunt looking at her disapprovingly and repeating over and over again that she would regret what she was doing.

"If I do," Mavina managed to say once, "I can always come back to England."

"If you have not spent all your money," Mrs. Lonsdale retorted sharply. "You will find it extremely expensive having to pay for everything yourself, which is something you have never done in the past."

"That is true," Mavina said, "but I am going to be very careful."

She had gone to the Bank the previous day and drawn out what she hoped was enough cash to get her to Calcutta.

She then asked the Bank to transfer what was left to a Bank in Calcutta.

They had given her letters of identification to show who she was when she arrived.

She felt she had been very business-like, just as her Father would have expected her to be.

When her luggage was piled on the carriage which was to take her to the ship, she was rather horrified by what it would cost her.

Her Aunt, being so annoyed with her, made no effort to accompany her.

"I would send one of the servants with you," she said, "but she would have to get back, and I do not expect you want to pay for her to do so."

"I shall be all right," Mavina said, "and thank you very much, Aunt Lucy, for having me to stay for so long."

"You are making a big mistake, as I have told you already," Mrs. Lonsdale said, "and when you come crawling back without a penny to your name, you will have to admit I was right."

Mavina did not reply because there seemed no point in it.

She merely waved from the carriage to her Aunt standing on the steps as she drove away.

'Now I am really on my own,' she thought.

When she arrived at Tilbury, her luggage was taken

aboard and she was shown the cabin she was to occupy.

It was, in fact, very small and dark, as it had no porthole.

As other people were coming aboard, the Stewardesses were far too busy to pay any attention to an obviously unimportant passenger.

Mavina sat down rather limply on her bed.

Then she thought she was being rather foolish and would enjoy seeing the ship move out of the Dock.

She therefore went up on deck.

There was still a large amount of luggage and big crates being taken into the hold.

There were people standing on the quay, looking at the ship, who were obviously just interested spectators.

On deck there were still many friends of those who were about to travel.

They were all talking animatedly, kissing and wishing those who were leaving "God Speed."

It was impossible for Mavina not to feel lonely as she moved along the rail.

Then a bell sounded for those who were not travelling to go ashore.

The staff on the *Coromandel* moved among the crowds on the decks, saying:

"All ashore, Madam, all ashore, Sir. The gangways will be drawn up in a few minutes."

They finally succeeded in getting the people who were not going with them off the ship and onto the quay.

Then, as the ropes were cast off and the ship started to move very slowly, everyone cheered and waved hats and handkerchiefs.

Mavina could see quite a number of the women were in tears.

'At least no-one is crying for me,' she thought.

Then, as they moved slowly down into the water, she turned to go back to her cabin.

It was then that a man whom she had not noticed beside her said:

"Good evening, pretty lady. Are we travelling together to India, or are you getting off at Alexandria?"

Mavina looked at him and saw he was a man about thirty, obviously not a gentleman, and somewhat over-dressed.

He had dark hair, brushed sideways from a neat parting.

She thought from the colour of his skin that he was not entirely English.

Because she thought it was bad manners to be rude, she simply replied coolly:

"Actually I am going to India."

"So am I," the stranger said. "As I think you are travelling alone, I am sure we can find ways to make the voyage very enjoyable."

There was something in the way he spoke and the expression in his eyes which made Mavina feel uncomfortable.

Without saying any more, she walked away, moving quickly with the people who were now going to their cabins.

She had almost reached the turning to her own cabin, when she found the man who had spoken to her was beside her.

"There's no hurry," he said, "and dinner is never punctual the night we sail. If you will tell me your name, I'll arrange that we are seated together."

"Thank you," Mavina replied, "but I prefer being alone."

She reached her cabin as she spoke.

Unlocking the door, she walked in and shut it behind her.

She was aware, however, that the man was still standing outside.

She thought before he went away that he gave a low laugh, as if he were amused.

chapter two

MAJOR the Honourable Willoughby Wicke was almost the last passenger to board the *Coromandel*.

He was received with the greatest respect by the Purser.

The Major was known to be on the Viceroy's staff and was a regular passenger aboard the P. & O. ships.

He was conducted to what was the best cabin on the first-class deck.

As the P. & O. did not have suites, it was understood that the Major always had the cabin adjacent to his adapted as a Sitting-Room.

This had already been done.

His Valet, who always travelled with him, would add a number of extra things to make it more comfortable.

The Major took it all for granted.

He was a tall and extremely handsome man who

looked and seemed to be older than he actually was.

He was very reserved about himself, and many people found him slightly awe-inspiring.

He was, however, known to the Viceroy and the Senior Commanders as one of their most efficient officers, and in fact, as they admitted amongst themselves, someone they could not possibly do without.

In London the Major was fêted and pursued by a great many beautiful women.

It was, however, beginning to be whispered about and recognised that no matter how alluring they might be, all their efforts to get his attention failed.

It was not that he did not contribute to any party at which he was a guest.

He was amusing and witty and, as his brother-officers knew, extremely intelligent.

What did seem strange, seeing how handsome he was, that however hard the gossips tried, there was never an *affaire de coeur* to gossip about.

As it happened, the Major was always whole-heartedly engaged in his work in India.

Although he was officially based at the Vice-Regal Residence either in Calcutta or Simla, he was often unobtainable.

Only the heads of the Army and the Viceroy himself knew where he was likely to be found.

What they did not know, and it would have interested them, was the reason for his fierce concentration on his work.

Even a light-hearted flirtation was something in which he never indulged.

The most beautiful ladies who visited India failed in their quest where he was concerned.

There were a great number of them, since the Viceroy, the Marquess of Dufferin, enjoyed entertaining.

Not only was Government House filled with guests, but there were parties for them every evening.

The Major never discussed his private affairs even with his closest men friends.

They were therefore left as curious as everyone else.

What had actually happened was a very sad story.

The Honourable Willoughby Wicke was the eldest son of Lord Cheswicke, the head of one of the oldest and most respected families in England.

The Cheswickes, who could trace their Family Tree back to the Saxons, had always taken part in public affairs.

The present Lord Cheswicke had been an admired and distinguished Statesman.

Then unfortunately ill-health forced him to retire to his country seat.

It was a magnificent house situated in five thousand acres of land about fifteen miles from London.

It had been built and rebuilt over the centuries.

In 1770 the Adam Brothers with their outstanding artistic genius had made it one of the most beautiful and distinguished-looking mansions in the whole country.

It was not surprising that Willoughby Wicke grew up to be very proud of the possessions which would one day be his.

He distinguished himself at Eton not only by being Captain of cricket but also Head Boy of the School.

His Housemaster was very eager he should go on to Oxford.

However, Willoughby insisted on going straight into the family Regiment, which was the Royal Horse Guards.

He was an outstanding rider and he knew that Army life was something which would really interest him and delight his Father.

He was at first posted in London.

It was not surprising that with his background, every ambitious Mama with a *débutante* daughter invited him to her parties and Balls.

He accepted many of them, and not surprisingly was a good dancer.

Then he fell in love.

Lady Lettice Byng was the most beautiful young woman of the Season.

She was not a *débutante*, and was nearly the same age as Willoughby Wicke.

It seemed strange, when she was so lovely, that she was not married, as she had expected to be, in her first Season.

However, family mourning had prevented her from being presented at Court for a year.

She had made up for the postponement by eclipsing every other girl that following Season, and sweeping the young men of the St. James's Clubs into an ecstasy about her.

She became engaged to the heir of the Duke of Lancaster.

Just before their engagement was announced, the Marquess had a very bad fall out hunting.

He was confined to bed with a number of senior Surgeons looking after him.

Lady Lettice did not join him in the North, but wrote to him frequently.

Although he was incapable of writing letters, he sent her passionate messages saying he expected to be with her in a very short time.

The months, however, dragged on.

Quite suddenly the young Marquess died when his Surgeons least expected it.

Lady Lettice was not exactly heart-broken.

At the same time, she realised that at nearly twenty-one she was at a disadvantage and out of place among the *débutantes* coming out every Season.

On the other hand, she was too young to fit in with the married women, who did their best to enslave the more important and handsome bachelors who frequented their dinner-parties.

When Willoughby Wicke fell in love with her, it seemed to Lady Lettice exactly what she required.

She accepted him without any hesitation.

Willoughby was in Heaven.

He had never been in love before, and he told himself he was the most fortunate man in the world.

His relations were delighted.

They did think, however, he might have been wiser to wait a little longer before taking up the responsibilities of a married man.

At the same time, Lady Lettice's family was as blue-blooded as theirs and, as they said to each other:

"She will undoubtedly make a very beautiful Chatelaine for Cheswicke Court when Willoughby inherits it."

The marriage was about to be announced.

In fact, the information for the Court Circular had already been approved, when Willoughby's maternal Grandmother, who lived in Devonshire, died after a short illness.

He was obliged to go to the funeral to represent his Father, who was advised not to travel so far.

It also meant that the young couple had to wait for a month before the announcement of their engagement could appear in the newspapers.

Willoughby went down to Devonshire and attended the funeral.

He said all the right things to the other mourners, then hurriedly returned to London.

He got back late in the afternoon and intended to go down to Cheswicke Court early the next morning.

Then, when he looked at the letters which were waiting for him, he found two which were particularly interesting.

One was a letter from his Commanding Officer, telling him he had been invited to become attached to the Staff of the Viceroy of India, who was then the Earl of Lytton.

He was to proceed as soon as possible to Calcutta.

There was obviously a sudden vacancy.

Perhaps someone had been killed or obliged to return to England.

Willoughby Wicke knew that did not concern him.

He had intended as soon as his engagement was announced to retire from the Regiment.

Lady Lettice had often said positively she had no wish to visit India or anywhere East of Suez.

Nothing was more important to him at this moment than that he should make her happy.

He pushed the letter to one side, thinking that he would answer it the next day.

Then he found a small parcel among his letters which was something he particularly wanted.

In the ecstasy of love he had told Lady Lettice that she was a star.

She shone brightly for him and he would follow her for the rest of his life.

She had smiled so prettily at him, and he had said that this would mean something very important to them both.

Because he was wildly romantic, he did not tell her what he was doing.

He went to the best jeweller in London and ordered a special star pendant to be made with the finest diamonds.

He opened the pink velvet box in which the pendant had been sent to him.

They had carried out his instructions with the expertise for which they were famous.

The star shone as if it were actually in the sky.

Hanging round Lettice's long neck and sparkling against her white skin, it would be a jewel worthy of her beauty.

Willoughby looked at it for some time, then suddenly he knew that he could not wait to give it to her.

She was expecting him back the following day.

They had already arranged that as it was the weekend, they would meet in the country.

He had told himself romantically that he would wait until they had dined together.

Her parents' house was only about three miles from Cheswicke Court.

He would then take her into the garden.

With the stars shining overhead he would pretend to pluck one from the darkness of the sky before he hung it round her neck.

He felt sure it would be a moment they would both remember.

As far as he was concerned, it would be engraved on his heart.

Then it struck him that the night was still young.

He had already dined with his Father, and there was no reason why he should not ride over to see Lettice and tell her he was back.

If she had gone to bed, she would come out on the balcony of her Bedroom.

Like Romeo, he would serenade her from below.

It would seem to him a part of his love.

He could imagine nothing more romantic than to climb up towards her, giving her first a bouquet of flowers.

He would take these from one of the greenhouses.

Then he would give her the star which she could put round her neck.

If she had gone to bed, her hair would be falling over her shoulders.

She would look, he thought, even lovelier than she did in the daytime.

Once he had thought of the idea, he immediately went into action.

He went to the greenhouse, where he knew his Father's finest and most exotic flowers were grown.

To his delight, he found that some orchids which had not flowered the previous year were now in blossom.

He picked them regardless of the fact that they were very rare.

It was intended they be seen first by ardent Horticulturists.

He added to them a few white lilies because they reminded him of Lettice.

Then, with the star pendant in his pocket, he went to the stables.

The groom on duty quickly saddled his fastest stallion.

Willoughby set off across country determined to reach Lettice in record time.

It took him a little longer than he expected, as the streams he had to pass were swollen.

Unexpected torrential rain had fallen in the middle of March.

He reached Lettice's home which was a somewhat

pretentious Victorian building.

The traditional family house belonging to the Byngs was in Northumberland.

The present Earl had agreed with his daughter that it was too far from London.

She was eager to be present at every Ball that took place in the city and a guest at every party that was given in the neighbouring counties.

The Earl was not being particularly unselfish, because he too wanted to be near London.

He was as it happened an obsessive gambler.

He gambled at White's and every club in St. James's, being on the whole a considerable winner.

What he had no intention of doing was retiring to the country to look after his Estate. He said he would be "bored stiff in the evenings."

What suited her Father suited Lady Lettice.

What she had told Willoughby before he left was that she would be waiting for his return in the country on Saturday night.

Unless the Earl had a large party, they could be alone together on Sunday.

As the gardens were particularly well kept, like those at Cheswicke Court, Willoughby rode almost on to the lawn at the back of the house.

He knew where Lettice's Bedroom was situated.

Tying his horse to a heavy garden seat, he walked towards it.

He was aware as he drew a little nearer that she was in her Bedroom and was awake.

There was just a faint light shining through the window which he thought would be the candles beside her bed.

He reached the house and looked up at the balcony.

It was a little higher than he had remembered.

He thought it might be difficult for her to bend over and take the flowers from him and the pendant.

Then at the side he saw there was a creeper trained to climb up the house.

It was doing so most effectively on a wooden trellis.

It was quite easy for Willoughby, who was extremely athletic, to climb up the trellis and the ornamental stone-work at the side of the balcony.

When he was holding on to the top of the balcony he thought he would call Lettice and tell her to come to the window.

Even as he drew in his breath he heard someone speaking.

He could not believe what he was hearing was true.

It was a man's voice deep and somewhat caressing.

Then, as he told himself the Bedrooms must have been changed and there were guests in Lettice's room, he heard her laugh.

It was a very soft and muscial laugh with which he was well acquainted.

She said, and he could just hear the words:

"You know you should not say things like that."

"Why not, my beautiful one?" the man replied. "And I have a great deal more to say, but it is easier without words."

There was silence, but Willoughby knew that Lettice was being kissed!

She was in bed with a man whose voice he seemed somehow to recognise.

For a moment he contemplated confronting them both and striking the man until he was unconscious.

Then he knew that he would not demean himself.

Very quietly and deliberately he tore the bouquet of flowers into pieces and dropped them on to the balcony.

Taking the pendant out of its pink velvet box, he put it into his pocket.

He placed the empty box on the balcony, where anyone opening or shutting the window could not fail to see it.

He slid down onto the ground and walked across the lawn to where he had left his horse.

He rode home slowly and thoughtfully.

From that moment every action he took in his life was to be deliberately thought out and considered.

Early next morning Willoughby Wicke returned to London and reported to his Commanding Officer at the Knightsbridge Barracks.

He had left early in a chaise drawn by four horses which he drove as well as he rode.

His Valet followed him with a large quantity of luggage.

Later that day, after saying goodbye to his Father and to no-one else, Willoughby Wicke left for India.

He never communicated again with Lady Lettice, and from that moment his life was changed.

When he arrived in India he did not waste much time amongst the staff at Government House.

He was interviewed by the Senior Officers.

Having had the report on him from London, they were well aware he was an exceptionally intelligent young man.

He was, in fact, just the man they were looking for at an extremely difficult moment.

Willoughby would disappear and return, reporting either to Calcutta or to Simla.

The reports he brought back with him were so exceptional that even those engaged in the secrecy of the Great Game could hardly believe them.

They realised that Willoughby was taking risks

which no other man would contemplate.

Yet by what seemed a miracle, he always survived.

The information he brought was of exceptional value.

It proved over and over again not only to be right, but it saved the lives of many British soldiers.

They were stretched to their utmost in trying to do what was asked of them at this particular moment.

By the age of twenty-seven, which he was now, Major Willoughby Wicke had become a veteran of the Great Game.

He had the confidence of men in high places with whom few young officers ever come into contact.

His secret work made him privileged to know the latest intelligence reaching India on Russian moves in the far North.

That he was a past-master at disguise went without saying.

He had just completed a very important and, of course, secret meeting at the War Office.

It had gone on until the early hours of the morning.

He had thought with relief he would be able to have a rest on the seventeen-day voyage to India.

Because he was of such importance, he was always invited to sit at the Captain's table.

He inevitably refused.

Occasionally he joined any friends who happened to be travelling at the same time for luncheon or perhaps a drink on deck.

The rest of the time he spent in his own cabins, waited on by his Valet.

As a relaxation he read the books he had no time to read when he was in India.

If he wanted exercise, he took it very early in the morning.

There were usually some outstanding athletes on board with whom he could play deck tennis.

If they were not available, he walked the decks when the other passengers were either eating or asleep.

As the *Coromandel* moved into the English Channel, he thought with a sigh that he could really relax.

The last week in England had been exhausting, to say the least of it.

He had been wanted by the War Office almost every minute of the day, answering questions, explaining what had happened, and, he had to admit, being listened to with respect.

If there was one person who seemed to understand what the Russians were doing, it was Major Willoughby Wicke.

The War Office Chiefs acknowledged this.

As the ship moved down the Channel, the Major realised it was going to be rough going through the Bay of Biscay.

This did not perturb him because he was an exceedingly good sailor and in fact had never been seasick.

He merely told himself sensibly that he had no wish to break an arm or a leg.

He would spend more time reading, which was undoubtedly good for his brain.

The *Coromandel* was, however, a very well-built ship and the pride of the P. & O. Line.

It pitched and rolled a little, but not half as much, the Captain said with pride, as her sister ships would.

By the time they neared Gibraltar, the sun was shining and the sea was blue, and the Mediterranean lay ahead.

Although it was the end of March, that evening was warm.

The Major, looking out of his porthole, decided he needed some air.

He walked, not onto the first-class deck, where he was sure there would be a number of men who would want to talk to him.

That would invariably mean they wanted him to meet their wives and daughters.

Instead, he climbed up onto the upper deck, where it was not usual for travellers to go.

Between the funnels and the super-structure, there was very little room for a seat and certainly not for deck-chairs.

The moon was shining and the sky was filled with stars.

There was little wind.

The Major moved slowly towards the bow, where he knew there was a seat protected from the wind, on which he often sat.

He reached it.

Then, to his surprise, as he came round the wooden partitions which protected it, there was a frightened scream.

He was aware of a woman sitting inside.

Because he knew he had surprised and obviously frightened her, he said quietly:

"I apologise for disturbing you, I did not expect to find anyone here."

He turned to move away, but the woman said:

"You are ... English ... oh, please ... please ... help me! I am ... frightened and ... I do not ... know what ... to do."

The Major was astonished.

His first thought was that this was no buisness of his.

Then he knew it was impossible to disregard the sound of fear in a very young voice.

"Yes, I am English," he answered. "What is frightening you?"

"It . . . is a . . . man," the woman replied.

The Major thought a little cynically it was what he had expected.

Yet because the voice was so young, he thought it was his duty at least to hear what was perturbing her.

He moved to sit down on the seat where he had often sat alone.

The woman to whom he had been speaking squeezed herself away at the other end of it.

"Now, what is worrying you?" the Major asked. "It cannot be right for you to be frightened on this very comfortable and pleasant ship."

"That . . . is what . . . I thought," Mavina answered, "but it has . . . got worse . . . and worse and . . . now I dare . . . not go back . . . to my . . . cabin."

There was a break in her voice which told the Major she was not far from tears.

Then, as he looked at her, the ship changed course a little and the moonlight was full on her face.

He could see that she was very young and extremely pretty.

He was also aware that there were tears in her eyes which were looking towards him.

Also tears were on her cheeks.

He waited, and after a moment Mavina said:

"He spoke . . . to me . . . first when I . . . came on . . . board and asked if . . . he could sit . . . next to me . . . in the Dining Saloon. I managed to . . . avoid that by . . . eating either . . . very early before . . . most of the

37

passengers . . . got there . . . or much . . . later."

She paused for a moment before she went on:

"Then . . . presents came to . . . my cabin. Flowers . . . chocolates, and . . . when I told the Stewardess . . . to take them back . . . to where they came from . . . she refused. The man must have . . . bribed her to . . . bring them."

Now the Major was frowning, but he did not say anything and Mavina went on:

"I had a . . . little peace . . . when it was . . . so rough, then . . . tonight . . ."

She could not go any further, and lifted her handkerchief to her eyes.

"What happened tonight?" the Major asked.

"I went to . . . the Library to find . . . another book, but it took . . . longer than I . . . expected because they . . . do not have . . . many books on India . . . which I . . . think is a . . . mistake."

The Major agreed, although he did not say so, and Mavina continued:

"When I got . . . back there was . . . a bottle of . . . Champagne in . . . my cabin . . . flowers and . . . something . . . to eat . . . but I did not . . . look to . . . see what . . . it was."

She gave a little gasp as she said:

"I knew . . . he meant to . . . join me and that . . . even if I . . . locked the door . . . the Stewardess could . . . let him in . . . so I ran . . . up here."

She added quickly:

"I know I ought . . . not to be . . . here because . . . this is for . . . first-class passengers . . . but I could . . . not think of . . . anywhere else . . . to go."

"I think it was very sensible of you," the Major said quietly. "This is something which should not happen on a decent ship. Now, tell me your name and the number of your cabin, and I will deal with it."

Mavina gave a little cry and said:

"Thank you . . . thank . . . you . . . I am sure . . . they will . . . listen to . . . you. I thought . . . if I went to . . . the Purser, he would . . . expect me, because I am of no . . . importance . . . to look . . . after . . . myself."

"You are travelling alone?" the Major asked.

"Yes . . . alone," Mavina replied. "Since there was . . . no-one to come . . . with me. I was determined to . . . go to India because I want . . . to find where . . . my Father . . . is buried."

She thought that sounded rather vague, and she added quickly:

"He was a soldier and was . . . killed in . . . action but the . . . War Office did not . . . say where."

"You have not yet," the Major said, "told me your name."

"It is Lonsdale, Mavina Lonsdale, and my Father was a Colonel in the King's Royal Rifles."

The Major stiffened, then he said:

"Are you saying your Father was Colonel Richard Lonsdale?"

"Did you know Papa?" Mavina asked.

"I met your Father only once or twice," the Major answered, "but I also know of the splendid work he has done and how brave he was."

"Oh, thank you for saying that!" Mavina cried. "I am sure Papa was . . . brave and the . . . Regiment will . . . miss him."

"I am quite sure they will, and a great number of other people will also," the Major said. "At the same time, you should not be travelling to India alone. Surely there was someone who could Chaperon you on the voyage, even if when you arrived you stayed with some members of your Father's Regiment."

39

"I had not thought of . . . doing . . . that," Mavina said. "Quite frankly, I have to make . . . my money last . . . as long as . . . possible, otherwise I shall have to go back to England without perhaps . . . finding out where . . . my Papa is . . . buried."

"So you are travelling alone and with very little money," the Major said as if he had to get it clear in his mind.

"I shall be all right," Mavina said quickly. "I was born in India and the Indian people are usually very kind."

"Yet I imagine the man who has frightened you is not an Indian," the Major said.

"No, but I think he is a . . . half-caste of . . . some sort and perhaps a . . . commercial traveller. It is very difficult to avoid . . . people of that . . . sort in the . . . second-class."

The Major knew this was only too true and that in the second-class Dining Saloon the tables at which the passengers ate were long and communal.

"Now I know you are your Father's daughter," he said. "I promise you this sort of thing will not happen again. Just give me the number of your cabin and stay here until I come back to you."

"It is 92B," Mavina said, "and . . . thank you. I was so . . . frightened and now . . . because you knew . . . Papa, I feel that . . . he must have . . . sent you to . . . help me."

"I am sure that is what has happened," the Major said quietly. "Now, just stay here, where no-one will see you until I return."

He rose as he spoke.

Silhouetted against the stars, Mavina saw how tall and broad-shouldered he was.

'I am sure that he is . . . very important,' she

40

thought. 'I am so . . . very lucky to have . . . found him. Thank you, Papa . . . thank . . . you.'

There were tears once again in her eyes, but she was no longer trembling.

She was quite certain as the Major walked away that her Father had heard her prayer.

The Major went to see the Purser, who listened to what he had to say.

He assured him that it was the sort of thing that was most deprecated on board and would not happen again.

He then agreed to everything Major Wicke asked for and sent a couple of Stewards to do what was required.

The Major went back on to the top deck.

Mavina was waiting for him.

She had wiped away her tears, and as she sat forward on the seat the moonlight was full on her face.

The Major could see again that she was very pretty indeed.

In fact, she was far too lovely to be travelling alone.

"I have made arrangements," he said, "that you will move into a cabin which is next to mine. It will take a few minutes for the present occupant to be moved."

There was a twist to his lips as he added:

"Fortunately it is a man who will not make a fuss, as a woman would do."

"I am . . . afraid . . . I cannot . . . afford to travel . . . first-class," Mavina said. "A dreadful thing . . . happened when we were told Papa was dead."

"And what was that?" the Major asked.

"Two months before he was . . . killed Papa drew every penny he . . . possessed from . . . his Bank in England. But no-one yet knows what . . . happened to it. I asked Papa's Solicitors to write . . . to India, but they said that the Bank there could . . . only say that he . . . had collected it from . . . them."

The Major thought this was very strange, but he did not say so.

Instead, he sat down again beside Mavina and said:

"Now, listen to me. I greatly admired and respected your Father, and one way the Army can thank him for what he did when he was alive would be to look after you. In the meantime, you are my responsibility and you will travel with me as my guest."

He spoke so firmly that Mavina knew there was no point in arguing.

She merely said:

"Oh, thank you . . . thank . . . you . . . now I need . . . not be . . . frightened . . . anymore."

"I shall be very offended if you are," the Major said, "and tomorrow I will ask someone on board to chaperon you until we reach Calcutta."

Mavina's eyes widened before she asked:

"Is . . . that . . . necessary?"

"I am afraid the gossips will think it is," the Major answered. "I have not introduced myself. I am Major Willoughby Wicke, attached to the Viceroy's staff, and therefore, as you can understand, I have to be very careful of my reputation."

He was smiling as he spoke, and Mavina gave a little laugh.

"In other words, you are . . . worrying about . . . mine," she said. "Thank you for being . . . so kind and, of course, it is . . . very exciting that I can . . . talk to you, if you can . . . spare the time . . . about India."

"You say you were born there?" the Major said. "Is that why you want to go back?"

"I wanted to go back to be with Papa," Mavina

said. "He had promised me that as soon as I left school I would join him. I think, because he insisted on my learning Russian, that he would have let me . . . help him."

There was silence as the Major stared at her.

Then he said:

"Help him? What do you think your Father was doing?"

Mavina moved a little nervously.

"Perhaps I should . . . not have said . . . that," she answered. "Papa never . . . talked to me about his . . . special work. But Mama told me once or twice how . . . frightened she was when he was . . . away from her and so I . . . guessed."

She looked at the Major as she spoke, as if she were afraid he would be angry with her.

"What do you think that work was?" he enquired.

There was silence.

Then, in a very small voice, because she felt she must answer, Mavina said:

"I think . . . he was . . . in the . . . Great Game."

chapter three

The Major took Mavina down to his cabins.

He showed her first his Sitting-Room, and then the cabin next to his which had been got ready for her.

It was a pleasant and comfortable first-class Bedroom.

After the small inside cabin she had occupied, Mavina thought it was almost like a Royal Palace.

"Thank you . . . thank . . . you!" she said. "It is so kind of . . . you to let me be . . . here and now I am no . . . longer afraid."

"You need be afraid of nothing," the Major said firmly. "Now go to sleep and we will talk about everything in the morning and decide what you will do when you get to India."

In the privacy of his room he thought Mavina was even more beautiful than she had been in the moonlight.

He was quite certain that she would find herself in a great deal of trouble if she tried to travel alone and wander about in India unaccompanied.

It was a problem that he took to bed with him.

He found it difficult to sleep as he thought what a daring adventure it was on the part of a young girl to go alone to India.

He also was thinking of what she had told him about her Father.

He wondered how it was possible that Colonel Lonsdale had thought his daughter could help him in the Great Game.

He was aware that, like so many other men who had taken part in the British secret organisation, Colonel Lonsdale had lost his life.

The British were aware that the Russians were determined sooner or later to invade India.

At the moment they were moving East and South, absorbing one after another the Khans of Central Asia.

They were building a railway across Siberia to the Far East.

Those in the Great Game had already informed the Viceroy the Russians were considering building a railway in Afghanistan.

This meant they contemplated the annexation of Tibet.

That country's southern frontier was actually within sight of Simla!

Everyone in the British Army in India knew that the Russians had occupied and then withdrawn from several remote outposts in the Hindu Kush.

It was they who supplied arms to and incited the savage tribesmen who lay behind the rocks and wadis of the North-West Frontier.

In the Great Game everyone who took part in it was known only by a number.

A most important aspect of their job was secrecy.

The Major, as it happened, had encountered Colonel Lonsdale on two different missions.

He was well aware how respected he was at Headquarters and what valuable service he had rendered before he retired to England with his wife and daughter.

Mavina had come back to look for her Father's grave, and that the Major could understand.

What he found incredible was that her relations should have permitted her to come alone.

He knew he would be failing in his duty as a soldier if he did not look after her.

But he was well aware, if it was known he was befriending a young girl, of the interpretation which would be put on it, especially by the women who had failed to capture his affections.

When the Major woke the next morning, he was already making plans and, as usual where he was concerned, they were minutely examined before he went into action.

He had breakfast in his Sitting-Room, but gave his Valet orders that Mavina was to have hers in her own cabin.

When breakfast was finished, and it was a light one, the Major went to see the Purser.

That official was even more apologetic than he had been the night before.

He had discovered, he told the Major, that the man who had pursued Mavina was a well-known troublemaker, and in future would not be allowed to board any ship of the P. & O. Line.

The Major accepted this without comment, then

asked for the passenger-list.

He read it carefully, and it took him some time before he discovered what he wanted.

The list was made out in alphabetical order, and it was not until he reached the letter "S" that the Major found the name of Suffolk.

Lady Suffolk was exactly the person he wanted to chaperon Mavina.

She was the widow of a Governor-General who had died ten years before and she was now getting on for seventy.

Every year she made what to her was a pilgrimage to India to see her old friends who were still alive and to stay for a short time at the Governor's house in Lucknow, where she had once spent five years.

She was a charming old lady, and whatever Viceroy was in office, she was always welcome on her arrival at Government House in Calcutta.

Because she had lived in India, Lady Suffolk had the habit of rising early in the morning, before the sun got too hot.

The Major found her sitting in a comfortable place on the first-class deck, in the garden-chair she had been asked to bring with her and which bore her name.

When the Major appeared beside her, she looked at him and smiled and held out her hand.

"I thought you might be on board, Major Wicke," she said, "and hiding yourself away, as usual, from those who want to see you."

"May I talk to you for a moment?" the Major enquired.

"Of course," Lady Suffolk answered. "Although I risk having my eyes scratched out by all the pretty women you are ignoring."

The Major laughed and signalled a Steward to bring him a chair.

He sat down and then told Lady Suffolk what had happened the previous night.

"It is disgraceful," she said. "At the same time, the girl should not be travelling alone."

"I understand," the Major said, "there was no-one to go with her, and she is determined to find her Father's grave."

"I think I remember meeting Colonel Lonsdale," Lady Suffolk said. "A tall, good-looking man with a very pretty wife."

"In which case," the Major said, "his daughter is like her, and, I am hoping, Lady Suffolk, that you will agree to chaperon her until we reach Calcutta."

"Of course I will, my dear boy," Lady Suffolk said, "but what are you going to do with her then?"

"I hope, if she could stay with you for a few days at Government House, I can persuade the Regiment to look after her and take her to where her Father is buried."

Lady Suffolk nodded.

"That sounds sensible. Now bring the girl to me, and of course I will arrange for her to have meals with me in the Dining Saloon."

"I am very grateful to you," the Major said. "I know you will understand that it would be a great mistake for anyone else on board to know what occurred when she very mistakenly tried to travel second-class."

Lady Suffolk smiled.

"It would make a very good story, especially that she was rescued by the tall and handsome Major Wicke."

49

The Major looked at her in consternation, and she smiled.

"Do not be afraid! I have kept a great number of secrets in my time, and no-one shall know of this except you and me."

"Thank you," the Major said, "and I will send Mavina to you very shortly."

Lady Suffolk's eyes twinkled as she realised he was determined not to be seen by anyone with a very pretty girl until they knew she was under her chaperonage.

Then, as the Major walked away, every woman on that part of the deck following him with her eyes, she thought it was sad that he was known by men for the brilliance of his brain but appeared never to be interested in women.

Lady Suffolk could not help thinking that it was a pity she was so old.

When she was young she had been an outstanding success, and it was always said no man could resist her.

The Major walked back to his own cabin and told his Valet to ask Mavina to join him.

She came hurrying at his command, looking, he thought, even more lovely in the daylight than he had thought her to be last night.

Now her eyes were shining and she looked excited and happy, very different from the pathetic, frightened little face he had seen in the moonlight.

"Good morning," she said as she entered the cabin. "I slept so peacefully and it has been wonderful to be able to look out of the porthole and see the blue of the sea. It is the colour of the Madonna's robe, just as I thought it would be."

"I am afraid you will find the Red Sea disappointing," the Major replied, "because it is not red."

Mavina laughed.

"Now you are being unkind to me," she said, "for being over-enthusiastic. But everything is so very different from what it was before, and I had a delicious breakfast."

The Major, who had risen as she came into the cabin, sat down and indicated an armchair next to his.

"Now, listen, Miss Lonsdale," he said. "As I told you last night, you should not be travelling alone, and I have found you a chaperon."

Mavina looked a little nervous.

"Is she nice?" she asked. "And was she very shocked that there was no-one with me?"

"Your chaperon's name is Lady Suffolk," the Major said. "Her Husband was Governor-General of Lucknow, and died ten years ago. But she comes back every year to see her old friends in India."

Mavina was listening intently and said:

"If she loves India, then I am sure she will be able to tell me lots of things that I want to know about it."

"That is what I thought," the Major said. "But it is very important from your own point of view that no-one except Lady Suffolk knows that you came aboard alone and that you had a disagreeable experience because you were travelling second-class."

Mavina looked at him, then she nodded her head.

"I am sure you are right," she said, "and that it should be a secret."

"Lady Suffolk has promised that it will be," the Major replied, "and she will never break her word."

"Once again I must thank you," Mavina said, "and I am very grateful."

"Then all you have to do is to enjoy the voyage and

forget that you began it on the wrong foot," the Major said briskly.

Mavina was looking at him without speaking and he knew perceptively there was something worrying her.

"What is it?" he asked.

"I know it is impertinent, if not tiresome, of me to ask for anything more," Mavina said, "but I was thinking, as I have nothing to do until we reach Calcutta, that I would like, if it is possible, to have some lessons in Urdu."

The Major looked surprised, and Mavina went on quickly.

"I used to speak it with Papa, but not, as you know, for some time, and I am very eager, when I do reach India, to be able to talk to the people in their own language, especially those who might have known Papa."

She thought the Major was looking sceptical, and went on again:

"Of course I do not want to worry you, but perhaps there is someone respectable among the third-class passengers who could give me lessons if they were not too expensive."

The Major was silent for a moment, and then he said:

"If that is what you really want, I think the best thing is for you to talk to me. For me Urdu is a second language, and we will talk it when we are alone together. Again, that is something which must not be known outside this cabin."

Mavina clasped her hands together.

"That is wonderful, absolutely wonderful of you!" she said. "But I do not wish to be a nuisance."

"I would not allow you to be that," the Major said with a smile.

"Then, thank you once again. It is something I always keep saying but can never seem to say enough."

The Major laughed.

"Now, I want you to go and talk to Lady Suffolk. She is sitting about three seats on the right from the entrance on the first-class deck. As she is nearly seventy, her hair is white, and she is wearing a blue frock."

Mavina got to her feet.

"I am sure I shall find her," she said.

She walked towards the door, and then she stopped.

"When can I see you again?" she asked.

"After luncheon. Lady Suffolk, like all sensible people who have lived in India, will lie down to avoid the heat. I shall be waiting for my pupil."

Mavina laughed, and it was a very pretty sound.

Then she slipped out of the room and the Major heard her running along the corridor.

"She is certainly original," he said to himself, then sat down at his improvised writing-desk to cope with the large collection of papers that were waiting for him.

Mavina enjoyed meeting Lady Suffolk and talked to her animatedly all through luncheon.

It was a very different meal from those she had eaten in the second-class Saloon.

As the Major knew, there the passengers ate at long communal tables with decanters on trays arranged over their heads.

According to who was travelling, the meal could be a very noisy one, or, as the man who pursued her intended, flirtatious and embarrassing.

Lady Suffolk, because she was old and slightly deaf, liked a table to herself, but she enjoyed having Mavina as a companion.

The Dining Saloon itself was decorated with potted plants.

There were spotless tablecloths on every table, and the waiters in white with small dark beards were extremely attentive.

Lady Suffolk was aware that a great many people were interested in seeing she had someone with her, and the men particularly looked at Mavina once, then looked again.

Being a good judge of character, she was soon aware that Mavina was completely unselfconscious and had no idea of her own attractiveness.

Quite a number of men who could not bother with Lady Suffolk before now came up to speak to her as the meal ended.

She introduced Mavina and said she was chaperoning her.

She liked the way she greeted the newcomers politely but made no effort to converse with them unless they addressed her directly.

When she went to her own cabin to lie down, Lady Suffolk thought that Mavina was both charming and unspoilt.

She was quite certain she was also very innocent.

'It is a pity,' she thought as her Lady's-maid undressed her, 'that Willoughby Wicke could not fall in love with someone like that.'

Then she remembered how many Beauties had failed dismally to capture him and knew it was an impossibility.

Mavina had run to her cabin to wash her hands, tidy herself, and went next door.

The Major was waiting for her and had an Urdu dictionary in his hands.

He had sent his Valet to find it in one of the Libraries on board.

It had turned up on the third-class deck and was somewhat dilapidated.

'At least,' he thought, 'it is better than not having one at all.'

However, when he talked to Mavina, he found she knew far more than he had expected.

He was used to visitors to India thinking they could speak the native language.

They could order a glass of whisky or some favourite Indian dish and tell the waiter to hurry up.

That really was all!

Mavina managed to keep up a conversation with him for five minutes, making only one or two mistakes.

"That is excellent," the Major said, "you speak very well."

"My Father was very fluent," Mavina replied.

The Major knew that it was extremely important for anyone in the Great Game to be able to impersonate different characters, also, to understand what was said to them by the ordinary Indian people.

When they had finished the half-an-hour which the Major had allotted for their lesson, he said:

"Now tell me how well you speak Russian."

"Not as well as I would like," Mavina answered, "but I can understand what is said to me. The teacher at my school, whom they had great difficulty in finding, was, when I left, quite pleased with my progress."

She gave a little sigh before she added:

'I thought . . . Papa would be . . . so pleased."

"I am sure he would have been," the Major said, "and, who knows, you may find it useful one day. I have always believed that any effort we make in improving ourselves is never wasted."

"I hope you are right," Mavina said. "But now I will not be able to work with Papa as I had hoped to do."

The Major thought it was very unlikely that Colonel Lonsdale would have taken her on "a mission."

If it was anything like those in which he had taken part, it would be extremely dangerous.

At the same time, Colonel Lonsdale must have had his reasons for wanting his daughter to learn a language that was certainly not heard in England.

He could only hope that it would not be completely wasted.

He was well aware from the way she had picked up Urdu that she was extremely intelligent.

He had also learned from their conversation that she had read a great many books on India.

There were some which he himself had found quite difficult.

He rose and went to the table standing against the wall.

On it there were a number of books his Valet had unpacked from his luggage.

"There are several books here," he said, "which I think will interest you and which you can borrow. I think you will find the one on the North of India interesting, and another which describes the author's attempt to climb the Himalayas."

"I want to read all your books," Mavina said. "Papa had a big Library and I thought it would last me all my life. But my Uncle insisted on most of it being sold with the house."

"That seems very unfair," the Major said.

"When one is poor and cannot pay one's own way," Mavina replied, "no-one listens."

The Major knew this was true but thought it very sad that someone so young had found it out so quickly.

Aloud he said:

"When we reach Calcutta, I will get in touch with your Father's Bank and see if I can learn anything about the money he had transferred there. You had better write down its name and anything else you know about it."

Mavina did as she was told, but she really knew very little.

She was convinced that her Father had invested the money in some way.

That was what she wanted to try to find out when she reached Calcutta.

The Major did not like to say it was like looking for a needle in a haystack, but he thought it.

Looking at him, Mavina said:

"I know you are thinking I am being optimistic, but I am quite certain we shall find what happened to Papa's money just as I shall find his . . . grave."

She paused for a moment before she added:

"You saved me last night when I was desperate; now I will never again doubt that Papa is looking after me and telling me what to do."

"Do you really think your Father would have liked you to come to India alone?" the Major enquired.

"I am quite certain that in some way he made my Uncle, who was very mean where money was concerned, leave me five hundred pounds," Mavina answered. "I would never have been able to start the journey without it."

She paused and looked up at the Major before she said:

"Then last night when I prayed to Papa to help me, suddenly you were there! Why should that have happened? I was alone and frightened and suddenly you thought you would walk on the upper deck."

She spoke so simply, yet, at the same time, with a sincerity which made it impossible for the Major to argue with her.

Instead, he said:

"I can only hope that you are successful in your mission."

"I am sure I shall be," Mavina said confidently.

They reached the Suez Canal and Mavina was fascinated by it: the great black-hulled ships with important-sounding names; their high structures, spick and span above the sand, and look-outs alert on their flying bridges, seemed somehow unreal.

There were Red Ensigns fluttering down the waterway.

She felt she was turning a corner of the world into a part that previously had been just a red blotch on the map.

By this time she had become accustomed to the luxury of the ship.

What was more exciting than anything else was that one could read in all the first-class cabins.

There was an arrangement by which electric light could be turned on and off at pleasure by the occupant.

Mavina kept turning the electric light in her cabin on and off because it was something she had never known before.

At home they had had oil lamps or candles.

The expense of installing electric light was, of course, for them out of the question.

When the ship reached the Red Sea it was getting much warmer but not yet unbearably so.

Lady Suffolk intended to spend a few days in Calcutta and then proceed to Simla.

That, she told Mavina, was what the Viceroy and Vicereine would be doing.

"It will be far too hot for you to stay in Calcutta, dear child," she said, "and you must ask Major Wicke where your Father's Regiment is, as I understand you will be staying with them."

Mavina could not help feeling a little frightened at leaving the Major.

She found it fascinating to have her lessons with him every day.

He also taught her in the evenings, when Lady Suffolk had retired to bed and she went to say goodnight to him.

He had learned from her, although she did not realise it, why her Father had left India.

It was because her Mother had been so frightened of his work in the Great Game!

She had insisted she could not stay alone being terrified he would never return.

The Major could understand this.

He could also understand why when his wife died, Colonel Lonsdale went back to his Regiment, who received him with open arms.

It was a tragedy, the Major thought, that he had been killed.

He was obviously executing some extremely difficult mission, perhaps on the North-West Frontier.

The Major saw difficulties ahead if the Colonel's body had never been found.

He might, in fact, have been presumed dead because he did not return.

There were many questions which concerned Mavina's pilgrimage.

The Major found himself lying awake at night, trying to solve a problem about which he had very little information.

He finally decided the best thing he could do was to take her first to Government House.

With Lady Suffolk's chaperonage he could arrange for her to stay there until he knew who was in command of her Father's Regiment and where they were stationed.

When he told Mavina what he had decided, her face lit up.

That was exactly what she wanted herself.

The Major was glad she was pleased.

At the same time, he thought it would be a great mistake if this child—which was how he thought of her—became so attached to him that it would upset her when they finally parted.

He did not expect her to fall in love with him.

That was a very different thing, and he was well aware such an idea had never entered Mavina's head.

'She looks on me,' he thought with a somewhat wry smile, 'as a Father figure and she is convinced that her Father actually sent me to her.'

The Major was well aware when a woman was beginning to find him irresistible.

He had seen the symptoms a thousand times: the look in her eyes, the invitation on her lips, the way she could not prevent herself from touching him with her long fingers.

He thought he knew every move, every expression, almost every thought.

There were none of these with Mavina.

She looked at him with wide-eyed admiration.

She listened to him with an attention that he found rather touching.

She read avidly every book her gave her, and discussed them with an intelligence he did not expect to find in a female.

At the same time, he realised she relied on him.

Now that she was nearing India, it seemed somehow larger and certainly more frightening than it had when she had been in England.

It was one thing to remember only the beauty of it when she had been with her Father and Mother.

The colour of the sky, the stars, the rivers, and the flowers seemed to flash before her eyes.

But she was still afraid after her encounter with the man when she came aboard, afraid that such a thing might happen again.

It was the Major who had protected her and saved her.

When he was not there and she was again alone, she wondered what would happen.

'Perhaps,' she thought, 'if I have to go on a long journey across India, I could pay some elderly woman to go with me.'

The Major had made it clear that travelling first-class on the ship and eating delicious meals in the Dining Saloon was his responsibility.

This meant that apart from the money she had expended on her second-class ticket, the trip so far had cost Mavina nothing.

It would be different, of course, when she left Government House and set off on her own.

'I shall have to be careful of every penny,' she told herself.

But her mind still persisted in thinking she should have someone with her when she travelled.

It was Lady Suffolk who told Major Wicke that her experience when she came aboard had made her afraid of men.

"What do you mean?" the Major asked.

He had joined Lady Suffolk after breakfast when her Lady's-maid had knocked on his door.

He had been told that her Ladyship wished to speak to him.

"Is there anything wrong?" he asked after he said "good morning" and a chair had been provided for him to sit beside her.

"If you mean has Mavina done anything wrong," Lady Suffolk said, "certainly not. She is without exception the most charming and delightful young woman I have ever met! I find her, which surprised me, extremely interesting to talk to. In fact, I think I have learned a lot since we have been together."

She laughed as she spoke, and the Major asked again:

"What is wrong?"

"I am just a little worried as to what you are going to do with Mavina after we arrive in India. As I have had daughters of my own, I realise that what occurred when she came aboard has made her frightened of men."

The Major looked astonished.

It was the last thing he expected Lady Suffolk to say to him, and the last thing he thought any girl as pretty as Mavina would feel.

"You will be surprised," Lady Suffolk was saying, "how many men have been pleased to see me or claimed acquaintance since Mavina has sat at my table."

The Major could understand this, and she went on:

"When Mavina made little effort to speak to them and refused to dance, which I found very strange, I finally understood. It was not shyness but fear that made her want to avoid them."

Major Wicke frowned.

"I suppose it is something that might happen," he said. "But I do not know what we can do about it."

"That is what worries me," Lady Suffolk said. "She is such a sweet and beautiful child, and I had hoped that she would find a Husband while she is in India. That would be a solution to all her problems."

She paused and then went on:

"I have the feeling that long before a man has a chance of proposing to her, she will run away from him."

The Major listened to what Lady Suffolk had to say.

Then, after luncheon, when he was talking to Mavina in Urdu, he thought she must have been mistaken.

They were laughing and talking quite naturally.

Mavina was even making jokes which was quite a difficult thing to do in another language.

Because the Major was sure Lady Suffolk was wrong in what she surmised, he said:

"When I discover where your Father's Regiment now is, I expect you will find it quite easy to reach them by train."

His work in the Great Game had taught him to watch the effect of every word on the person to whom he was talking.

He knew that instantly Mavina stiffened.

"Will I . . . have to go . . . far?" she asked.

"I have no idea until we reach Calcutta," the Major replied. "The Regiment may be quite near or it may be in the North. I should think the latter is most likely."

He was aware that Mavina drew in her breath.

Then she said in a small voice:

"Do you think it would be very expensive for me to hire a Chaperon or perhaps an . . . elderly courier?"

The Major knew now by the way she had said the last two words that Lady Suffolk was right.

"I am sure," he said, "that I can find someone with whom you can travel so that you will be looked after and not alone."

The light was back in Mavina's eyes.

"It would be wonderful if you could do that," she said.

There was a little pause.

Then in a voice that was obviously nervous Mavina asked:

"You do not . . . think you will be . . . going North too. If that is . . . where I have . . . to go."

"I think it most unlikely," the Major said.

Then, as he saw the expression on Mavina's face, he felt as if he had hit something small and defenceless.

chapter four

WHEN the ship arrived at Calcutta punctually at the time expected, Mavina was thrilled to find that a special carriage escorted by a detachment of Cavalry had been sent to collect the Viceroy's guests.

With Lady Suffolk and the Major, she drove through the crowded streets.

The women looked beautiful in their saris, and the sun covering everything with a beautiful golden haze made Mavina feel she had stepped back in time.

She was in the India she remembered as a child.

Because she was excited, her eyes were shining, and both Lady Suffolk and the Major were moved by her enthusiasm.

"It is lovely! Lovely!" Mavina cried. "Just as I remembered it, and it is like being in one of my dreams."

She felt this was more than true when she arrived at Government House.

Her Father had told her and so had the Major, speaking in Urdu, the story of what was undoubtedly the finest Governor's Palace in the world.

It had been the young Irish Peer, Richard Wellesley, Earl of Mornington, who in 1798 had arrived in Calcutta as Governor-General.

He brought with him, as all Governors did, stores, carriages, and baggage valued at two thousand pounds.

But less than a month after his arrival, the Earl decided that the existing Government House was not important enough for him.

It was, in fact, no different from the houses of the leading citizens of Calcutta.

He therefore ordered that it should be pulled down and a Palace erected on the site.

The building started in 1799.

By that time the Governor-General was engaged in a very serious war against Tipu Sultan.

After Tipu was defeated and killed, the Earl, as a reward for his success, was created the Marquess of Wellesley.

His younger brother, Arthur, played a very prominent part in the war.

He was to become later the famous Duke of Wellington.

With this victory in the background, the Palace that was rising in Calcutta became a symbol of the growth of British Power.

The Directors, however, of the East India Company were furious four years later.

They learnt the cost of the building was 63,291 pounds.

In fact, they thought it was a shocking extravagance on the part of the Marquess of Wellesley.

Yet Government House was actually worth every penny of its cost.

It dominated the Calcutta scene in a way no other building did, and everyone who entered the House found it fascinating.

Mavina was no exception.

She was thrilled with the huge rooms, and very impressed by the servants in their red and white uniforms who bowed whenever she appeared.

Because her Mother had taught her a great deal about furniture and china and glass, she admired the magnificent collection of lustres.

She was shown a gilded seat that had belonged to Tipu Sultan.

The Louis Seize chairs and settees for the State Drawing-Room, adjoining the Ballroom, had been given to the House by a previous Governor-General.

What she had also learned from the Major, which amused her, was that the Kitchen was two hundred yards away from the house.

The food had to be put into *Dhoolies*, or boxes on poles, which were carried on servants' shoulders.

"In fact," the Major said, "the Marchioness of Dufferin said soon after her arrival 'the Kitchen is somewhere in Calcutta but not in this house.' "

Mavina looked wide-eyed at the Viceroy when she met him.

As the Major could see, she was somewhat overawed by his importance.

He was nice-looking, with a curly moustache and a trim beard.

He also had an unmistakable charm and was very quick-witted.

This was part of his mixed Irish and Scottish blood.

He was a man of the world, cultured and charming,

and also a Diplomat with a talent for literature.

Although Mavina was somewhat awed by the Viceroy, she found the Marchioness absolutely charming.

She made Mavina think of her Mother.

Harriot had married the Marquess, who was fifteen years older than she was, because she loved him.

She had forced herself to overcome her natural shyness.

She was determined to be a suitable wife for a man who obviously had a brilliant career ahead of him.

She had managed, although no-one expected it, actually to enjoy State occasions, and to say the right thing to all manner of people.

She acquired a dignity and grace.

She had by now the reputation of being one of the most fascinating great ladies of her time.

There were few people who were not prepared to say that Harriot Dufferin was the perfect Vicereine.

The Marquess was not only the perfect Viceroy, but one of the greatest public servants England possessed.

Mavina felt that the huge Government House could not be real and neither were those inhabiting it.

The Major watched her.

He thought she played her part perfectly as the young girl coming for the first time into contact with the grandeur of the East.

As soon as he was alone with the Viceroy, the Major learned that a crisis was brewing with Russia.

"I suppose, Wicke," the Marquess said, "that having been at sea, you are not aware of it, but the sooner you help me, and I badly need your help, the better."

The Major knew that, as usual, when there was a crisis, the Viceroy was in his element.

"Tell me, Your Excellency, what has occurred since I left England," he said.

"The Russians," the Viceroy answered, "who are continuing, as you know, to infiltrate into Central Asia, are now proceeding to occupy the district of Panjdeh, which the Afghans claim to be part of their territory."

The Major was instantly aware of the danger.

Panjdeh was dangerously near the Afghan city of Herat.

No-one knew better than he that the British had guaranteed "the integrity and independence of Afghanistan."

They were, therefore, bound, if the Afghans required them to do so, to drive the Russians out of Panjdeh by force.

All this passed through his mind as he said aloud:

"This might cause an Anglo-Russian war."

"Exactly what I was thinking," the Marquess said. "But I have one trump card I may be able to play."

"What is that?" the Major asked.

"The Amir of Afghanistan, Abdur Rahman, has agreed to pay me a State visit in the Punjab. I am going there the day after tomorrow."

"I am sure your Excellency will manage somehow to avert a catastrophe," the Major replied.

"I am hoping I can do that," the Viceroy said. "At the same time, Wicke, I need your help to find out what is happening on the North-West Frontier. Those who have managed to get through have warned us that the Russians are stirring up trouble."

"That is nothing new," the Major replied. "As it happens, I intend anyhow to go in that direction because I have promised to find the grave of Colonel Lonsdale."

The Viceroy nodded.

He had already learnt why Mavina was in India.

If anyone could discover where her Father was buried, it would be Major Wicke.

"I believe," he said slowly, "that Lonsdale had been on a secret mission to Peshawar. The information and maps he brought back have since proved invaluable."

The Major thought it was what he had expected.

Yet he still had to get information as to where the Colonel had been buried.

When he left the Viceroy, he went in search of Mavina.

A plan was forming in his mind which he thought he must soon put into action.

The Viceroy was going to the Punjab and it was now April.

It was obvious that he and the Vicereine would go on to Simla, where they always stayed during the summer months while it was so hot.

There was nothing that Mavina could learn in Calcutta.

The Major had already found out that her Father's Regiment was not at the moment in the North.

It had moved down to Kanpur.

He suspected that the Commanding Officer could not tell her anything more about her Father's death than she knew already.

The Major, however, had found that in the Great Game it was the biggest mistake to talk about what he was going to do.

He just did it, and then if the information was obtainable, spoke of it later.

As he went to find Mavina he was trying to decide what it would be wisest to keep to himself.

He could not find her in the large Reception rooms.

There were some of the Viceroy's guests talking to each other and at the same time sipping cool drinks because the heat was increasing.

He went to one of the windows which opened onto the garden.

It was then he saw, to his surprise, Mavina running swiftly towards the house.

It was something no-one except a girl as young as she would do while the sun was shining.

He stepped out to meet her.

As she saw him, she swerved from the direction in which she was running.

It was only as she reached his side that he realised from the expression on her face that she was upset.

However, he did not wish anyone in the room he had just left to be aware of it.

He therefore took her arm and led her quickly towards the shade of some tall trees on the other side of the lawn.

He was aware as he did so that she was trembling.

When they sat down on the comfortable seat on which the servants had arranged soft cushions, Mavina said:

"I . . . wanted to find . . . you and . . . suddenly . . . you were . . . there."

"What has happened?" the Major asked in a quiet voice.

"It was . . . foolish of me . . . very . . . foolish," Mavina said, "but I went into . . . the garden with . . . a man. He interested . . . me because he was . . . talking about . . . the Regiments in India and . . . I thought I might . . . learn something I did not know . . . about Papa."

"And what happened?" the Major asked.

He thought he knew the answer and, as he ex-

71

pected, Mavina looked away.

The Major waited.

Then she said in a very small voice:

"The man . . . and he was . . . quite old . . . tried to . . . kiss . . . me."

It was what the Major expected, and he said:

"You must be aware that you are a very pretty girl. If you are so indiscreet as to go alone into the garden with a man, you cannot be surprised if he takes the opportunity of kissing you."

"But I never . . . thought . . . I never . . . imagined that he . . . would . . . think of . . . me like . . . that."

The Major smiled to himself, and said in the same quiet voice:

"It is, you must realise, a compliment. If you were ugly and wore spectacles, he would in all probability have ignored you completely."

"I see what you mean," Mavina said, "but I wanted to . . . talk to . . . him seriously."

"And he wanted quite naturally to kiss anyone so pretty and leave any serious talk for someone plainer."

Now Mavina laughed, although it was a little shaky.

"I know . . . you are . . . thinking," she said, "that I am very . . . silly and I should have . . . thought of all this before I came . . . alone to . . . India."

"Instead of which, you are learning the hard way," the Major said. "Let me tell you that most girls of your age and with your looks would be offended if a man did not want to kiss them."

Mavina looked at him in surprise.

"I thought," she said, "that . . . one only . . . really wanted to kiss . . . someone when . . . one was . . . in love."

"I think most young women would find that very restricting," the Major said.

"But I would hate . . . anyone to . . . kiss me unless I . . . loved them," Mavina said. "If . . . that is what is expected . . . out here in India . . . then I have been . . . rude to one of His Excellency's . . . guests and he may be very . . . angry with . . . me."

"What did you do," the Major asked.

"I was so surprised when he tried to kiss me," Mavina answered, "that for a moment I did not believe it was happening. Then, just as . . . his lips were about to . . . touch mine I . . . hit him . . . hard in . . . the . . . face and . . . ran away."

She looked at the Major nervously as she spoke.

She was sure he would be terribly shocked at her behaviour, but to her surprise he was not.

"If he tried to kiss you," he said, "without preparing you for what he was about to do, then he deserved all he got. Forget him."

"Can . . . I do . . . that? Or ought I to . . . apologise?"

"Not unless you want him to try again," the Major said.

Mavina gave a little cry.

"No . . . of course . . . not. But I will be very . . . careful in future . . . not to go in . . . the garden . . . alone with . . . anyone."

She spoke humbly, and then the Major was aware she was thinking.

After a pause Mavina said in a very small voice:

"What will . . . happen to . . . me when . . . you and . . . Lady Suffolk are not . . . there?"

"That is a question that I also have been considering," the Major said. "Since the Viceroy is leaving the day after tomorrow, we must leave too."

Mavina clasped her hands together.

"You said 'we'! Can I go . . . somewhere with . . . you?"

"We are going to find your Father's grave," the Major said, "which I am quite convinced, although I am waiting for confirmation, is in the North-West of this country. It is where I have to go anyhow on the instructions of His Excellency, so you can come with me."

He saw Mavina's face light up almost as if the sun were shining through it.

Then she said:

"That will be wonderful! Simply wonderful! I have been praying that I would . . . not have . . . to leave . . . you."

The Major did not answer, but merely rose to his feet.

Then, as Mavina rose too, he said:

"We will go back to the house, and I expect Lady Suffolk has finished her rest by now. If not, sit down beside one of the other ladies in the Drawing-Room. But do not talk to them or anyone else of where we are going or what we are doing when we leave here."

"No, of course not," Mavina answered.

She knew it was an order.

She told herself that if the Major was going on a mission of some sort, then she must be very discreet, and, in fact, be careful of every word she uttered.

She remembered what her Mother had told her.

When her Father was playing a part in the Great Game, he would never confide even in her what he was doing, but somehow she guessed.

"It was the way he looked, the way he spoke," Mrs. Lonsdale said, "which told me without words he was going into danger."

74

"You did not ask him any questions, Mama?" Mavina enquired.

"It would have been useless if I had," her Mother replied. "Your Father was completely dedicated to his work and this particular aspect of it was to him sacred."

"What happened when he went away, Mama?"

"He would kiss me and say 'take care of yourself, Darling,' " her Mother answered. "And then almost before I realised what was happening, he had gone. I sometimes had weeks to wait alone, desperately afraid, very frightened, and without the slightest idea of where he was."

"You did not speak to any of the other officers or their wives about it?" Mavina asked.

"No, of course not," Mrs. Lonsdale answered. "They just thought he had been sent for by some Commanding Officer in a different part of India."

She sighed before she added:

"I am completely convinced that no-one in the whole camp had the slightest idea of what your Father was doing."

"It was very brave of him," Mavina said.

"Too brave," her Mother answered. "When I made him take you and me back to England, I always felt that I had deprived him of something very important in his life, and however hard I tried, I could not make him forget."

Mavina thought of this now.

She told herself that if the Major suddenly left her alone in some strange place, she must not complain nor must she ask too many questions.

She was quite certain that those who took part in the Great Game never confided in anyone, otherwise her Father would have told her Mother what he was doing.

'All the same,' she thought, 'I am quite certain Papa would have let me help him, even if it was in only a very small way.'

Yet maybe if she was with him, no-one would suspect he was doing anything dangerous.

As soon as they had come in from the garden, the Major disappeared.

It was a servant who opened the door for Mavina to go into the Drawing-Room.

She told herself that he did not wish the women sitting round the room gossiping to know that they had been together.

"He does not ... want to be ... involved with ... me," she told herself, "and I must be very careful not to be an encumbrance. At the same time, how can I possibly do without him?"

She could see now what a wild idea it had been to come here alone!

To think she could move about India without attracting the attention of men.

The man on board the ship had been particularly unpleasant.

But she had never imagined that sort of thing could occur in Government House.

'Perhaps I should try to make myself look ugly,' she thought.

She contemplated buying spectacles, as the Major had mentioned them.

Then she knew she wanted to look her best so that he was not ashamed of her.

She was wearing one of her Mother's gowns at the moment.

It compared well with the gowns worn by the other

women staying at Government House.

One of them had just arrived, and Mavina thought that she was very beautiful.

She had hair that was more red than golden and her eyes had just a touch of green in them.

Everybody greeted her warmly when she appeared, so she was obviously very well known.

By listening as they talked to her, Mavina gathered her name was Lady Flora Prentice.

'She must,' Mavina thought, 'be about twenty-five or a little older.'

Then she learned, to her surprise, that Lady Flora was married.

"Is your Husband with you?" one of the elderly women asked as she shook hands with her.

"No, the poor Darling is in England," Lady Flora replied. "The Prime Minister says he cannot do without him."

Someone laughed at this and said:

"Apparently you can! I assume, Flora, you are on your way to Simla."

"Of course," Lady Flora answered. "How could I miss the most fascinating house-party of the year and the most perfectly *romantic* surroundings."

She accentuated the word "romantic."

Mavina thought that everyone laughed in a somewhat cynical manner.

It was then that the door opened and three officers came into the room.

One of them was the Major.

Lady Flora turned round and saw him.

She gave a cry which seemed to echo across the whole Drawing-Room.

"Willoughby!" she exclaimed. "I thought you would be here. How wonderful to see you!"

She moved towards him with the grace of a ship moving over the water and held up both her hands.

The Major lifted them one after the other to his lips.

"I expected you to turn up sooner or later, Flora," he said. "Like a bad penny, or one that is misbehaving."

Lady Flora laughed and looked up at him from under her dark eyelashes.

"And I presume," she said, "you are still the iceberg that you were when I left you."

"But of course," the Major answered. "What else could you expect in this climate?"

Lady Flora slipped her arm through his.

"One day you will melt," she said, "and think how amusing that will be."

"I will promise you one thing," the Major replied, "it will not be in Simla."

Everyone laughed at this, although Mavina did not understand why.

She only thought that Lady Flora, looking up at the Major, was quite obviously infatuated by him.

It gave her, although she did not understand why, a strange feeling in her breast.

'He likes her,' she thought, 'and who can blame him? She is so very pretty.'

She then corrected her words to "beautiful."

There was something about Lady Flora that made her different from all the other women.

When a little later Mavina was alone with Lady Suffolk, she asked her if she had met Lady Flora before.

"Oh, a great many times, my dear," Lady Suffolk replied. "Flora has been coming to India ever since she was a teenager, and was just as pretty then as she is now."

"Did all the men fall in love with her?" Mavina asked.

She thought perhaps the question was rather impertinent, yet it was something she wanted to know.

"Of course they did!" Lady Suffolk said. "She was always a very naughty girl even when she was very young, flirting with the young men and leading them on. And when they wanted to marry her, laughing at the very idea."

"But she is now married?" Mavina asked.

"Yes, to a very intelligent and charming man who is the Leader of the Government in the House of Commons."

"He let her come out to India alone?" Mavina enquired.

"I do not think Flora would ever be alone for more than ten minutes," Lady Suffolk replied. "The men buzz round her like bees round a honeypot."

Again Mavina thought how pleased Lady Flora had been to see the Major.

Again there was that strange and rather painful feeling in her breast.

'Perhaps he loves her,' she thought, 'and that is why he has never married.'

But she had called him an iceberg.

She wondered if that meant what she had hoped it did.

At dinner that evening there were a number of people dining at Government House.

It seemed to Mavina as if Lady Flora held them all spell-bound.

She was sitting on the right of the Viceroy, but many other people seemed to be joining in the conversation.

Those who were not talking were listening to what she said.

She was flirting with the Viceroy, and Mavina could see he was amused by her.

The Major was on her other side and she was flirting with him also.

Mavina, who was much further down the table, could not hear what they were saying.

However, Lady Flora was obviously making the Major laugh.

She looked lovely.

Mavina thought it was not surprising that every man at the table was watching her.

She was wearing a tiara of emeralds in her red hair and a necklace of the same stones was round her neck.

It seemed to Mavina that her dress was cut very low.

In fact, she was sure her Mother would have been shocked by it.

It made Lady Flora's white skin even more noticeable.

When she moved across the room, she had a grace that made her appear as if she were a nymph from the sea or perhaps a goddess from one of the mountains.

When Mavina went to bed, she could only think of Lady Flora and the amused expression on the Major's face when he was listening to her.

When dinner had finished, there was an orchestra playing in the Ballroom.

A number of people came into Government House from outside.

Standing beside Lady Suffolk, Mavina was hoping that the Major would ask her to dance.

Then, when she thought he had not yet come from

the Dining-Room, she saw him talking to Lady Flora.

She thought he must have gone straight to her when the Gentlemen joined the Ladies.

There were already three other men standing beside Lady Flora, listening to her and laughing at what she said.

And all, Mavina thought, completely and absolutely captivated by her.

Then, as the orchestra began a dreamy waltz, she saw Lady Flora move forward.

She seemed to melt into the Major's arms.

Her head was thrown back as she looked up at him.

Mavina thought no couple could look more attractive, or and she forced herself to say the word, romantic.

She turned to Lady Suffolk and said:

"I have rather a headache. Would it be very rude if I went to bed?"

"That is just where I am going," Lady Suffolk said. "If that is what you want to do, my dear, we will slip away together."

She saw the Vicereine at the other end of the Ballroom and added:

"Nobody will worry if we are not here, and personally I need my beauty sleep."

They went out of the Ballroom and climbed the stairs to where their Bedrooms were close together.

"I think, dear child," Lady Suffolk said when they reached their rooms, "you should really be dancing with all those nice-looking young men who are downstairs. Are you quite certain you want to go to bed?"

"Yes, that is what I . . . want to . . . do," Mavina replied.

Lady Suffolk kissed her.

She knew exactly what Mavina was feeling and why.

When she had gone into her own Bedroom and Mavina had gone along the corridor to hers, Lady Suffolk sighed.

'It is inevitable,' she thought, 'that every woman he meets falls in love with Willoughby Wicke. It is just because he eludes them that they find him irresistible. But Mavina is different. He will break her heart and she will not understand why it is broken.'

Down below, the Major was, in fact, aware that Lady Suffolk and Mavina had left the Ballroom.

It never occurred to him that he might be the reason that Mavina had gone to bed.

He thought that, because she was afraid of men, she had not wished to dance with anyone.

"The sooner I find her Father's grave," he told himself, "and send her back to England, the better."

It was difficult for one so young to understand.

But in the heat of India, and with a large number of young men with not enough to do, love affairs were a daily occurrence.

They were, in fact, accepted as something quite natural.

He himself found Simla, with its *affaires de coeur* following one after another, rather a bore.

He could understand that for women who had put up with the humdrum day-to-day life of their Husbands' Barracks, it was an escape.

But he knew after his experience with Lettice it was something he did not want himself.

Mavina would have been surprised if she had heard his conversation as he danced with Lady Flora.

She had asked him to dance with her while three

other men were waiting for her to decide whom she would choose.

She was being mischievous, partly as she always was, also partly because for years she had pursued the Major in her outrageous manner.

She could not understand why, like every other man, he did not find her irresistible.

"Now that you are back, Flora," he said, "for Heaven's sake behave yourself, and do not break too many young Subalterns' hearts. Last year Ravenshaw very nearly committed suicide."

"He was very emotional," Lady Flora replied, "but, you must admit, very good-looking."

"If you behave so badly this year," the Major said, "I shall tell the Viceroy to ban you as being a danger to the Army in general."

Lady Flora laughed.

"You know as well as I do, Willoughby, I would much rather be flirting with you than with these beardless boys."

It was the kind of outrageous thing she would say, and the Major merely replied:

"I am far too busy to have you on my hands as well as a great many more important things."

"What could be more important than me?" Lady Flora demanded. "And you know, dearest man, it would be very amusing if you agreed to slip away with me to some secret place where no-one would interrupt us."

"There are no secret places," the Major replied, "which are not known to those terrible women with their long tongues in Simla."

"If I find one they do not know, will you come with me?" Lady Flora enquired.

She looked up at him as she spoke, looking so

lovely that the men round the Ballroom watching her held their breath.

The Major, however, answered:

"You know the answer to that. If I did go away with you, I assure you the only thing I would give you is a good smacking, which is what you have deserved ever since you left the cradle."

Lady Flora laughed.

"If you did that, it would assure me that at least you are capable of some emotion where I am concerned! But at the moment I am just afraid the icicle has got even colder."

The Major smiled, but he did not reply.

Looking up at him as they swung round slowly to the music of Johann Strauss, Lady Flora said:

"What would you do if I kissed you passionately at this very moment?"

"I advise you not to risk it," the Major replied. "I should be tempted to spank you very hard and insist that the Viceroy send you back to England on the next boat."

"I really believe you might do it," Lady Flora said. "Let me tell you, Willoughby Wicke, you are the most annoying, infuriating, and exciting man I have ever met."

"Thank you," the Major said.

He suddenly stopped still.

Lady Flora realised he had brought her back to the three men she had been with when she had asked him to dance.

The Major looked at them.

"I return Her Ladyship to you," he said. "She is an excellent dancer, but do not believe a word she says to you."

He walked away and Lady Flora looked after him, then stamped her foot.

"That is the most infuriating man," she said to those who were looking at her, "that I have ever met in my whole life."

The Major walked out of the Ballroom to his Bedroom.

His Valet was waiting for him, a man who had been with him for some years and whom he could trust completely.

As the Major appeared, he jumped up from where he had been sitting on the floor, polishing a pair of his shoes.

"You're early, Sir," he said.

"I know, Hill," the Major replied. "But I have had enough."

"There's a note come for you, Sir, 'tis on the writing-desk."

The Major walked across the room to where the desk was standing by the window.

On it was a small and rather crumpled envelope with his name on it.

He opened it quickly and read the very short message inside.

It was what he had been waiting for and confirmed what he already suspected.

Slowly he lifted the envelope and its contents to the top of one of the lighted candles which stood on the desk.

When it had burned to a cinder, he turned towards his Valet:

"We will leave, Hill," he said, "tomorrow morning."

The man who was half Indian and half English nodded.

"Anything you require specially, Sir?"

"Just bring what I usually require for me and Miss Lonsdale and the bag I gave you just before we left England."

"Very good, Sir," Hill replied.

The Major then lapsed into silence.

Only when Hill had extinguished all the lights in the room did he say as he reached the door:

"Good night, Sir. The usual time in th' morning?"

"Yes, as usual," the Major replied.

When he was alone he found it was so hot that he wondered if he should go up and sleep on the roof.

It was something he often did when the heat was unbearable.

Then he thought it was too much trouble.

He merely threw off the sheet which was covering him.

He had expected to fall asleep at once.

Instead, he found himself thinking of Mavina and wondering if he was making a terrible mistake.

Now that he knew where her Father's grave was, should he be taking her to see it?

Perhaps if he were wise, he would tell her that it could not be found.

Her Father had been killed by the Russians outside India and she must therefore go home.

Then he had the uncomfortable feeling she would still persist in trying to find her Father's grave, wherever it was.

As things were at the moment, she might easily walk into danger without realising it.

It was not going to be easy, he thought, to take her there.

At the same time, it was somewhere he had to go to himself.

The Viceroy had asked for his help in this unexpected crisis.

The Major was quite certain that if it was humanly possible, the Marquess, with his brilliant diplomacy, would somehow avoid an Anglo-Russian war.

Yet no-one knew better than he did that it would be touch-and-go.

Therefore, he could hardly refuse to play his part as effectively as was possible.

Then the Major shut his eyes and let his brain work like a machine almost on its own.

He could see quite clearly, almost as if someone were pointing it out to him, exactly what he should do.

It would not only please the Viceroy but also satisfy Mavina.

Then, as if everything had settled itself without his forcing it in any way, the Major fell asleep.

It was something he had taught himself to do at will.

Sometimes when it would have been exceedingly dangerous for him to be unconscious he had to go for days, if not weeks, with very little sleep.

Now what troubled him had been solved and he slept quietly without moving.

Then it was morning and Hill was calling him.

chapter five

WHEN Mavina left Government House the next morning, she felt she was setting off on a great adventure.

They drove in state with the mounted escort on either side of them to the Station.

Vaguely Mavina remembered it, but it seemed to her now even bigger and more impressive than it had been when she was young.

In Indian cities the largest and most ornate public building was usually the Railway Station.

In Calcutta the main Station was second only to Government House.

The architect's imagination had led him to produce domes and clocks, mock-oriental caravanserais, and an immense glass and girder roof.

The British were tremendously proud of the railway system they had built in India.

It had, in fact, been a tremendous achievement to

enable people to travel by train from Calcutta to Peshawar by 1885.

To Mavina, the confusion at the Station was as fascinating as if she were in a theatre.

There were an enormous number of Indians in *dhotis* and saris, turbans and swathed torn rags.

Some wore baggy white shorts, and there were invariably nose-clips and ankle-bangles on the women.

Moving about on the platform were soldiers in scarlet uniforms, Priests in yellow robes, and Englishmen in topees and bush-jackets.

There were wide-eyed hawkers shouting in hollow voices.

They peered through the windows of the railway carriages, begging the passengers to buy their wares.

Everywhere Mavina could see entire families sleeping, feeding babies, or sitting on piles of luggage which were tied up with string.

Because the Major was so important, there were servants from Government House to sweep the *hoi polloi* to one side.

They escorted them to where the British Station-Master was waiting at the end of the platform wearing a dark blue uniform and looking like an Admiral.

Mavina had already learned that the British Ladies and Gentlemen always travelled first-class.

They usually had a servant in the compartment next door.

Waiting for her and the Major was a very superior Drawing-Room carriage with two Bedrooms and a Pantry.

The upper-class Indians, she learned, travelled second-class.

Mechanics and commercial travellers, whether British or Indian, went intermediate.

At the very back of the train were the fourth-class carriages in which travelled the ordinary Indians, squashed like sardines on the slatted wooden seats.

For journeys which even now took longer than a day, the Sahib and his families took their own tiffin-basket, which was refilled at every stop.

There were Refreshment Rooms at most junctions.

The upper-class English, however, did not leave the train.

Their food was brought to them, having been ordered in advance.

The Major had done this, or someone at Government House had ordered it for him.

Mavina was fascinated when as the train drew into a Station, men in white would leap out of the shadows carrying their luncheon or dinner on trays covered with a napkin.

This was an immediate service.

She soon learned, however, that she had to eat very fast because before the train left, the waiters wanted the plates back.

They were frightened in case the great engine should steam off before the plates were back in their keeping.

When Mavina said goodbye to the Viceroy, he had said a few words on one side to the Major.

She had wondered what it was about.

She had the uncomfortable feeling that he was being told to do something very special and secret, in which case it would undoubtedly be dangerous.

Then she told herself she was being imaginative and tried to settle down to enjoy the journey.

The British had built first the Great Trunk Road.

It was the principal highway which ran direct from

Calcutta through Delhi and Lahore to Peshawar in the Punjab.

It took, when it was finished, three months to travel up the Road to the furthest point of the country in the North-West.

Then, when a railway system was developed, everything was changed.

Now the Great Trunk Road had huge British railway engines clanking from one side of India to the other in a very short time.

There was a turbaned Sikh fireman sitting in the tender with his pile of logs.

Behind him was the long line of the train with its four-wheeled wagons at the back raising a cloud of dust.

There were closed passenger-carriages, crowded with white-robed travellers standing on the couplings, hanging on to the doors, and even crouching precariously on the roofs.

To the Indian the Government's steam trains seemed to be carrying them on their way to glory.

The Major had told Mavina that the journey would take some time.

They should therefore take a few books with them to read in case they got bored with looking at the countryside.

Following his advice, Mavina chose three books from the large Library at Government House.

She promised the Librarian she would return them.

Yet once they had started on their journey, she found that the Major talked to her and answered all the questions she had been longing to ask him.

The books, both hers and his, remained unopened.

There seemed so many things to discuss.

They were quite surprised when the train came to

a standstill and they found their luncheon or their dinner was being brought in.

When finally Mavina went to bed in her comfortable compartment, she thought it had been the most interesting day she had ever spent.

"He is so wise and so experienced," she told herself. "I am so lucky to have him to talk to."

She thought how different it would have been if Lady Flora were with them.

She felt a cold shiver run through her.

The beautiful woman he had been dancing with last night haunted her.

The next day passed in much the same way, except that Mavina had a quick look at the roofs and domes of Delhi.

They reached Lahore in the Punjab the following day.

That evening, after they had finished dinner and the train was once again moving on, the Major said to her:

"I have something special to say to you, Mavina."

She looked up at him, and he went on:

"We are now getting to a dangerous part of our journey. I have learned that your Father's grave is actually on or near the Fort which guards the Khyber Pass."

"You are . . . sure Papa's grave . . . is there?" Mavina asked.

"That is what I have been told," the Major replied. "But you understand, because you have read the history of India, that the Khyber Pass is one of the most dangerous entrances to India."

Mavina made a little murmur, and he continued:

"The Russians are always making trouble for us by stirring up the tribesmen and giving them orders."

"Yes, of course, I have read about that," Mavina said, "but I am very excited to hear that you have found Papa's grave."

"I cannot say positively that I have found it," the Major replied, "but I understand that is where he died, and where I am sure the British will have buried him."

Mavina gave a deep sigh, and the Major added:

"As I have already said, there is considerable danger in our approaching it, and I think it would be a mistake for us to go there looking as we are now."

Mavina stared at him in astonishment.

"Do you ... mean we ... should go ... in disguise?" she asked.

"That is what I am suggesting," he said. "So before we arrive at Peshawar tomorrow at about two o'clock, I want you to change your clothes, and I will change mine."

He lowered his voice as he went on:

"We will get off the train quickly and mingle with the second-class passengers, who, as you are aware, are only two carriages behind us."

Mavina felt a little bewildered although she did not say so.

She waited until the following morning after breakfast.

Then he asked her to go to her Bedroom, where Hill had laid out some clothes she had never seen before.

They were not clothes that a Lady of Quality would wear.

They were the clothes, she thought, of a woman who was not rich and who could by no means aspire to travelling first-class.

Hill was obviously a past-master at this sort of thing.

94

He arranged her hair in a different way, then placed on her head what she thought was a rather ugly white sun-hat.

She certainly looked very different from when she had stepped aboard the train at Calcutta.

When she went into the Drawing-Room and saw the Major, she gave a gasp.

It was not that his clothes were particularly unusual, but he seemed in some magical way of his own to have changed from looking like a handsome, aristocrat of importance to being a rather ordinary man, the type one might see moving about any large city in England and not give a second glance.

He wore a pair of dark spectacles which hid his eyes.

His hair was brushed in a different way and she thought he looked not only less important, but somehow older.

As she went towards him he said to Hill:

"That is excellent, and now, Mavina, let me introduce myself: I am Doctor Eric Robinson and I come from Manchester. I am in India on a holiday combined with a certain amount of business."

Mavina could only laugh.

At the same time, she felt there was a serious undertone to all this which she did not quite understand.

"You will be leaving your luggage in the charge of Hill," the Major was saying. "He will not be coming any further with us, but will wait at Peshawar until we return."

Mavina was surprised, but the Major continued:

"Tell him the bare necessities you want to take with you, and he will pack them so that I can carry them with my things in one suitcase."

Mavina thought he would think her tiresome if she

asked a lot of questions now.

She therefore went back into her compartment and told Hill what she thought she would require.

"How many nights do you think it will be?" she asked.

Hill shrugged his shoulders.

"I imagine two, Miss," he replied, "but one never knows with th' Major."

"I am sure of that, if nothing else," Mavina answered, thinking he was a continual surprise.

As the train steamed into Peshawar, there was a huge crowd on the platform.

The usual Indian families with many children sitting on their luggage were there.

Porters with heavy bags, children screaming, and a number of goats also littered the platform.

These were later to be tethered in the guard's van and would provide fresh milk for the first-class passengers.

As the train puffed very slowly to the end of the platform, the Major suddenly jumped out.

He pulled Mavina after him, and took the suitcase and what looked like a Doctor's leather bag from Hill.

He slipped along the side of the train to join the crowd of passengers emerging from the second-class.

It all happened so quickly that Mavina felt she could hardly draw breath.

Then she was being jostled and pushed by all the people moving towards the entrance doors.

The Major kept with them.

She thought he managed to melt into the crowd and did not look of any importance, whereas in Government House he had stood out, even amongst the other important guests of the Viceroy.

With some difficulty they managed to secure a rickshaw which was waiting for hire outside the Station.

Instead of giving the address of a Hotel, Mavina heard the Major say:

"The Dak bungalow which is on the road to Rawalpindi."

The man driving the rickshaw whipped up his rather tired horse, and they set off.

It was impossible to speak in his hearing in case he understood English.

They therefore drove in silence.

About a mile outside Peshawar they came to what Mavina recognised as a Dak bungalow.

These bungalows were little more than a small box rather than a house, with a verandah to keep it cool.

Over the years some of the Dak bungalows had been enlarged and become more impressive than they were when first introduced by the British.

This one was now obviously facing competition from Hotels, which were springing up inside Peshawar, and the *Khansamah* was surprised to see them.

"I am Doctor Robinson," the Major introduced himself, "and I and my wife wish to stay with you tonight."

"I am very honoured, *Sahib*," the *Khansamah* replied.

"As my wife has a cold," the Major went on, "I would like, if possible, two rooms."

The *Khansamah* bowed even lower.

"Impossible, *Sahib*. Only two in Bungalow and Artist who is painting pictures of our country in one."

The Major frowned as if this were something he had not expected.

The *Khansamah* then said:

"Two beds *Sahib*, you be very comfortable."

Before the Major could reply, he showed them into a narrow Bedroom.

It contained two *charpoy*—Indian beds—covered with mosquito netting, but there was no bedding on them.

"I am afraid," the Major said, "as I did not expect to be in Peshawar for more than one night, I have no blankets or quilts with me."

"I find, *Sahib*," the *Khansamah* said, "I find, you very comfortable."

The Major knew this meant he would be charged extra for things which were usually required by travellers who did not have servants with them.

He ordered supper in another room which was used as a communal Dining-Room.

Then, when the *Khansamah* left, he walked across the room to where Mavina knew there was the washing-place.

It was, as he expected, very primitive with buckets of water standing beside the sluice.

He also noticed that instead of a door into it, there was only a curtain made of beads.

Mavina was taking off her hat in front of a mirror which was hung on the wall.

The Major came close to her.

"Be careful what you say. The washing-place is connected to the one next door, and it is always possible to hear what is said between the two."

Mavina smiled at him.

"I will be very careful."

"I am sorry about the Bedrooms," the Major said quietly. "This place, because it is so ramshackle, is, I believe, usually empty, but we leave tomorrow morning."

"I am sure we can manage," Mavina said.

She felt shy because she was sharing a room with him.

At the same time, the mosquito nets over the beds made her feel they would be isolated from each other.

She also knew that the Major must have a very good reason for their staying in this place rather than Peshawar itself.

When she had taken off her hat and the jacket which went with her plain dress, she felt cooler.

The Major said he had ordered drinks for them on the verandah.

She went out eagerly because it was exciting to be alone with him.

Creepers had grown up and around the verandah, and it smelt fresh and herbal.

Behind the bungalow was a compound, but it was untidy and dusty.

Again Mavina could not help wondering why they had to go to such a strange place merely because they were visiting the Fort.

They sat talking, and there seemed to be a great deal to say.

They spoke in low voices so as not to be overheard.

Later they went into the small, ugly room in the centre of the bungalow.

There was no-one else there.

Mavina gathered, while they were eating their meal, that the other visitor to the bungalow was having his food in his Bedroom.

She felt that the Major was curious about him, but he did not ask any questions.

They ate the dull and rather unimaginative food that was put in front of them.

The Major drank, as was expected, Indian beer, while Mavina had some lime-juice.

"As we shall be leaving fairly early tomorrow morning," the Major said, "perhaps about half-past nine, I suggest you go to bed. If you undress first and get into bed, I will try not to disturb you."

Mavina look at him nervously.

"You are not . . . going away . . . from the bunga-low?"

She had a sudden fear that he might go off somewhere.

She would then find herself alone without the slightest idea of what she should do.

"I promise you I will not do that," the Major said, "so do not be frightened."

"I am not frightened as . . . long as . . . you are . . . there," Mavina said. "But it is all rather strange."

"Of course it is," he answered. "I cannot explain now, but it would be a mistake to travel to the Fort looking like ourselves."

He spoke in a very low voice and glanced over his shoulder before he did so.

Mavina knew instinctively that he did not really want to take her to the Fort.

If she were sensible, she would not insist on their incurring all these difficulties.

At the same time, she told herself she must see her Father's grave.

Having come so far, she could not go away from India without, in her own way, saying goodbye to him.

The Major unexpectedly put his hand over hers.

"Do not worry," he said, "let me do the worrying. Just go to sleep and I promise I will not be long in coming to bed."

"I am trying to do . . . exactly what . . . you tell . . . me," Mavina said.

"You are being very brave and sensible," the Major said as he smiled, "and I give you full marks."

Mavina laughed.

Then she got up and went to get ready for bed.

She undressed and washed from the buckets of cold water.

She thought it would be easier if she had someone to tip them over her.

She managed, however, to get clean and cool.

Then, putting on a thin, pretty nightgown which had belonged to her Mother, she got into bed.

The *Khansamah* had made up each bed with a rather lumpy mattress, a sheet, and one blanket.

The pillow was fairly hard, but it had a clean cover.

Mavina snuggled down, and because she was really tired, she fell asleep.

She woke up with a start and did not realise at first where she was.

She wondered why she could not hear the rumble of the train's wheels.

Then she remembered she was in the Dak bungalow and she was aware that the Major was asleep in the other bed.

She could just see him because the curtains did not fit over the windows.

The moonlight was streaming through the sides of them, and Mavina knew the sky would be brilliant with stars shining like diamonds over the world.

She knew they would look even lovelier up there than they had in Calcutta.

She slipped out from under the mosquito net, and tiptoeing silently across the floor, went to the windows.

She pulled back the curtains only a little in case she woke the Major.

Then she looked out, and she realised nothing could look more beautiful.

The rocky land which drifted away into a far horizon was transformed by the moonlight into a fantasy of silver.

It was so lovely that she stood for a long time looking at it.

Finally she told herself she must go back to bed.

It was then she was aware that there was a man approaching the verandah.

She wondered if he was another customer coming to the bungalow.

On this side there was no entrance to the balcony.

Anyone wishing to enter the bungalow had to go round to the front.

To her surprise, however, the man, as he reached the creeper-covered wall, climbed over it.

She thought for a moment that he might turn and come towards the window from which she was peeping.

Instead, he turned left and went to the room next door.

Again to Mavina's surprise, he climbed through the open window.

It seemed to her rather strange.

Then she thought that he was, of course, the man who was occupying the next room and whom they had not seen.

He must have gone for a walk in the moonlight, as she would have liked to do.

She let the curtains fall back into place.

As she did so, she was aware that her hands were hot, and she suspected that the curtains were not too clean.

She walked towards the wash-room.

She was very careful not to let the bead curtain jingle, as it might have woken the Major.

The window in the wash-room was uncurtained.

She could see quite clearly her way to where the pails of water were standing.

Then, as she bent towards them, she heard voices.

As the Major had warned her, the two wash-rooms were not separated from each other.

As she listened she could hear quite clearly one man talking in a low and somewhat gutteral voice.

Then she stiffened and drew in her breath, because he was speaking in Russian!

The Major was fast asleep.

He had in his usual way relaxed completely, determined not to worry about tomorrow until tomorrow came.

Then suddenly his mosquito curtain was pulled aside and something soft, warm, and terrified flung herself on his bed.

For a moment it was hard for him to believe what was happening.

Then in a whisper he could hardly hear, Mavina was saying breathlessly against his ear:

"He is . . . going to . . . kill us . . . he is . . . going to . . . kill us . . . both before . . . we leave and . . . they are . . . attacking the . . . Fort . . . at Midnight . . . tomorrow."

She was trembling violently as she spoke, and the words came from her lips in jerks.

The Major put his arms round her.

He was aware because he was naked to the waist that her heart was beating frantically against him.

"It is all right," he said very softly, "I will not let anyone kill us. Tell me what happened and how you know this."

"They were . . . talking in . . . Russian," Mavina murmured.

He felt the tremor that went through her.

"Slowly," he said, "tell me about it slowly."

"I went . . . to the . . . washing-room," Mavina answered, "because my . . . hands were hot . . . then I . . . saw this man . . . climb over the . . . verandah and go . . . into the . . . room next . . . door."

She paused for breath.

"You could not see him clearly?" the Major asked.

"No . . . but I . . . thought he . . . must be . . . the English artist . . . we were . . . told is . . . staying . . . here."

"But you heard him talking?"

"He was . . . talking in a very . . . low voice but I . . . could . . . hear what . . . he said."

"And you understood him?"

"I . . . understood when he . . . said, 'Tomorrow at . . . Midnight we will . . . attack the . . . Fort. The bomb . . . has been . . . placed on the . . . North-West Rampart and . . . when it . . . explodes we will . . . burst in . . . through the gap . . . and annihilate . . . them all.' "

Mavina's voice trailed away because she was completely breathless.

The Major said, still very quietly:

"It was very clever of you to hear that. Now tell what else he said."

"He said . . . to the . . . other man, 'Are you . . . alone here?' and he . . . answered, 'No, there . . . are two . . . English . . . a Doctor and . . . his wife.' "

Now Mavina trembled even more violently than she had before.

The Major could feel it against his body, and his arms tightened.

"What did the other man say then?" he asked.

"He said," Mavina whispered, " 'Kill them . . . before you . . . leave. They might . . . be dangerous . . . one never . . . knows.' "

"He will not do that," the Major said. "Because you have been clever enough to save us both."

"How can . . . you stop . . . him? He may . . . shoot us or . . . stab us."

"He will do neither," the Major said, "and now I want you to be very quiet and not move or be frightened at anything I do."

"What . . . are you . . . going . . . to do? If you . . . try to prevent . . . him he may . . . kill you . . . first. Oh, please . . . let us . . . run away."

"I do not think that would be possible," the Major said, "and as your Father's daughter you know it is something we cannot do."

Mavina was silent.

The Major put her very gently to one side and got out of bed.

She saw he was wearing a cloth round his waist and his chest was bare.

He moved across the room so silently that she knew it was something he must have learned in his training in the Army.

He opened the small leather bag which she thought looked like a Doctor's.

She expected he would take out a revolver.

Instead, he drew out a yellow silk handkerchief and tucked it into the top of the cloth he was wearing.

Then stealthily he moved across to the washing-room.

She knew he was listening to hear if the Russians were still talking to each other.

Then he came back into the room.

He stood for a moment by the bed on which she

was sitting, and looked down at her.

Then he put his hand on her shoulder.

"Remember," he said, "you are your Father's daughter. Do not move or speak until I return."

He opened the door as he spoke and went out.

Mavina knew with a feeling of horror where he was going.

"But how," she asked herself, "how can he be so foolish to go without a gun and without a dagger to challenge a Russian of all people?"

It was with the greatest difficulty she stopped herself from jumping up and running after him.

She wanted to beg him, if necessary on her knees, not to do anything so foolish!

"How can he go just as he is?" she asked.

She felt as if the whole ceiling were falling down on her head.

As it happened, although naturally Mavina was not aware of it, the Major had taken with him the most dangerous weapon in the whole of India—the *Rumal*.

The gentlemen of the East India Company had not originally intended to govern India, but merely to make money.

They were determined not to interfere with Indian customs, especially religious ones.

They turned a blind eye to the rumours and legends of Thuggee.

Then India became part of the British Empire.

The British did not merely conquer or exploit their subjects, they always tried to reform them.

The Thuggees were dedicated to Kali the blood goddess.

Black and ferocious with her noose, her sword, and her bludgeon stuck all over with human skulls.

Her temple was in Bindachal.

The Thuggees enjoyed the secret protection of rich men and Rajahs, Moslem as well as Hindu.

It was the most ancient secret of India, and Binda-chal was the priesthood of the cult.

There, once a year, the stranglers went to receive their sacred instructions and to pay the priests of Kali.

The Thugs worked in absolute secrecy according to strictly enforced rituals.

They murdered travellers on the highway, stran-gling them from behind with a silken noose.

They cut the bodies of their victims with ritual gashes, threw them down wells, or buried them.

They burnt all their belongings which were of no value to them.

When they left, not a trace of a Thug or a traveller was to be seen.

One of the most dangerous things the Major had ever done was to join those who went to Bindachal to worship the goddess Kali.

He had learned the Thug secret language which en-abled them to talk to each other in the presence of strangers.

The *Rumal* was the yellow silk handkerchief tied round a silver rupee with which the stranglers killed their victims.

The *Pola* was the secret sign left by one Thug for another.

The *Gobba* was the round grave of a Thuggee in which the corpses were laid, never to be found.

The Major learnt that after every murder the Thugs ate sacramentally a morsel of consecrated sugar.

When he left Bindachal he was to all intents and purposes a Thuggee with an expertise which any one of them would envy.

The English were determined to put down the

Thugs, because in 1812 over 40,000 people were murdered by them.

It had taken a long time, but now, though their work was greatly reduced, it was impossible to keep track of every traveller all over the country, or to be certain of what had happened to those who had disappeared completely.

Very softly the Major turned the handle of the door to the room where he knew the Russian was sleeping. . . .

When he came out as slowly and silently as he had gone in, he opened the door of his own Bedroom.

Just inside, Mavina was kneeling on the floor, her hands over her face.

For some seconds he just stood looking at her.

He knew she was praying.

It was a long time since he had seen a woman praying with such intensity that it was agony.

Then, although he had made no sound, as if she was aware of his presence, she looked up.

For a moment she could only stare at him as if she could hardly believe it was true and he was there.

Then swiftly as a bird flying from a tree, she sprang to her feet and ran towards him.

She flung herself against him.

"You . . . are . . . back . . . you . . . are . . . back!"

The words seemed to come not from her lips but from deep inside her trembling body.

Then, holding on to the Major, she burst into tears.

He held her close against him.

Then he said very quietly:

"It is all over, and I want you to go to sleep for as long as you can, because tomorrow we have to warn the Fort that they are to be attacked."

"He . . . did not . . . hurt . . . you?" Mavina asked.

"As you can see, I am quite unhurt," the Major said, "and that is one Russian who will not worry us again."

"You . . . killed . . . him?" Mavina murmured.

The Major could feel her tears on his bare skin.

"Forget him," he said, "he is unimportant. You and I have to finish the job that your Father was doing, and we must not make any mistakes."

"Can . . . we do . . . that?"

The Major smiled.

"It is what we are going to do."

He picked her up in his arms and carried her to bed and laid her down on it.

"Try to sleep," he said, "we must have all our wits about us tomorrow."

"You are . . . not leaving . . . me?" Mavina asked.

"I am here just beside you," the Major said.

He pulled her mosquito net to and then went across the room.

He put the yellow silk handkerchief back into the leather bag.

Then he got into his own bed and shut his eyes.

chapter six

MAVINA felt she had been asleep for only a few minutes before the Major was touching her shoulder and telling her to wake up.

She forced herself to open her eyes.

They were so heavy that it was almost impossible to do so.

"What . . . is . . . it?" she asked.

"We have to be on our way," he said, "so get up and dress."

It was an order, and she responded to it as he moved away.

She dressed herself quickly, realising it was only just after dawn.

The sun was just beginning to rise in the sky.

The Major appeared when she was putting on her plain white hat.

"There is something to eat, which is not very appetising, in the Dining-Room," he said. "But at least the coffee is drinkable."

She smiled at him, and he said:

"For a woman, you are very quick."

He picked up her nightgown as he spoke and put it into the suitcase.

He followed it with her brush and comb.

Mavina looked round quickly to see if she had forgotten anything, then went with him into the Dining-Room.

She ate what was prepared because she thought it was what the Major expected.

When she had finished, he led the way outside, carrying the suitcase and his Doctor's bag.

As she followed, she saw to her astonishment a *Tika-Gharri* was waiting for them.

She had always thought there was nothing funnier than a native cart which she remembered looked like a box on wheels.

That was what her Father had told her it actually was.

A flat piece of wood was fastened overhead to serve as protection from the sun.

There was only just room enough for two people to sit inside and very little space for luggage.

Mavina knew that a *Tika-Gharri* was so light, it could travel faster than any other horse-drawn vehicle in the whole country.

The one that was waiting seemed somewhat weather-beaten.

The blue with which it had been originally painted had faded, and there were several cracks in the sides.

At the same time, the wheels looked strong.

The horse which was pulling it was, she saw, a slim-legged and sure-footed Northern breed.

These were known to be reliable on long distances and mountain roads.

Then, as the Major got into the *Tika-Gharri*, she realised that he was driving.

She thought it was strange, but did not make any comment.

The *Khansamah* was bowing and scraping ceaselessly.

This told Mavina that the Major must have paid him well for their night's stay at the Dak bungalow.

Only as they drove off and were out of hearing did she say:

"How did you ... manage to be allowed to ... drive this yourself?"

The Major smiled.

"Its owner was exceedingly frightened and refused point-blank to drive us to the Fort. However, he let me take his horse, provided I paid enough for it."

It was not important, but he thought there was no-one better at extorting money from a traveller than the Indians who provided them with transport of any sort.

All that mattered was that they should reach the Fort alive.

He and Mavina had to save the garrison from being taken by surprise at Midnight.

When they set off, the road was at first wide and smooth.

Very shortly ahead lay a dim, flat plain.

Only on the horizon were there the peaks of mountains.

On the road they passed frontiersmen who strode by with long, lifting steps.

More than once camels came sailing through the

dust, moving towards Peshawar like ships to port from a distant sea.

The camel-bells tinkled merrily, then grew fainter and fainter.

Again Mavina and the Major seemed alone in an empty world.

She realised he was driving with great expertise.

She supposed he was used, in England, to a team of four horses, and was certain he would handle them brilliantly.

It would have been a mistake to talk.

She knew that he was urging the horse forward, not only by his driving but with his will and every instinct in his body.

They had left what there was of civilization behind, and the road was now much rougher and bordered by rocks.

These seemed to increase rapidly in size until there were mountains on either side of them.

The land was no longer flat, nor was the road dusty.

Mavina had no idea that the Major was remembering what had been repeated so often in England and in Calcutta about the North-West Frontier.

"The rocks and wadis," the Viceroy had said to him just before he left, "are where the savage tribesmen lie in ambush. With the Afghans brooding behind the tribesmen, and behind them the Russians."

The Major knew he was gambling on the chance that all the tribesmen had been told to attack the Fort at Midnight.

None of them, therefore, would wish to alert the garrison by firing pot-shots at unimportant passersby.

The Major also knew that no Englishmen of any importance would travel in a *Tika-Gharri*, and he hoped the eyes watching them would think they were not worth a bullet.

But still it was a gamble.

Only when he saw the Fort ahead of him did he feel he could breathe more easily.

By the middle of the day the sun had grown very hot and Mavina had longed to ask if they could stop for a little while in the shade.

She had known, however, by the expression of determination on the Major's face that it was something he would not wish to do.

She could feel without his saying anything how eager he was to reach the Fort ahead.

The Major had stopped once to let the horse drink at a road-side stream.

But it was only a few minutes grace and then they were on their way again.

Then, at last, with the sun shining through a curtain of golden hazes onto the mountains behind it, Mavina could see the roofs and walls of the Fort.

It was built on the plan of all Britiish Forts, encircled by a mud wall and standing on high ground.

Any enemy who approached it would be at a disadvantage.

There was a steep climb before he could reach even the outer walls.

"We have ... done it! We are ... here!" Mavina said aloud.

Her voice sounded hoarse because she was tired.

Her throat seemed still to have the dust in it which had enveloped them when they first left the Dak bungalow.

Even as she spoke, she had an unmistakable feeling of danger.

It was almost like a presentiment that they would

not reach the safety of the Fort.

For the first time since they had left, the Major applied his whip on the back of the horse.

It hastened its pace until the fragile little *Tika-Gharri* swayed from side to side.

The rumble of its wheels on the hard ground grew louder.

Mavina felt as if they were being pursued and only speed could bring them safely to the security of the Fort.

She held on to the sides of the cart so as to keep her balance on the hard wooden seat.

'Why . . . should I be . . . frightened,' she asked herself, 'when . . . everything . . . seems so . . . peaceful?'

Then, because she knew instinctively what the Major was feeling, she found herself praying.

"Please, God . . . please let . . . us reach the . . . Fort safely," she said in her heart. "Please . . . God."

They were climbing and climbing.

She held her breath lest at the last moment the danger she sensed so vividly from the Major should materialise in the shape of a bullet.

Then the horse turned for the last time.

Ahead was the massive nail-studded gate leading into the Fort, with two sentries standing just inside it.

The Major drove in through the open gate.

A soldier carrying a rifle came to the side of the *Tika-Gharri*.

"Who are you and what do you want?" he asked in English.

"Take me immediately to Colonel Stephenson," the Major said.

The Major spoke in an authoritative voice, and the soldier recognised it.

He moved to let them pass.

The soldiers in the compound looked at them in surprise, then moved forward as if to speak to them.

The Major drove straight on until they came to the inner building of the Fort itself.

Here they were challenged by another sentry, and again the Major demanded to be taken to the Colonel.

He stepped out of the *Tika-Gharri* as he did so, and helped Mavina to her feet.

Then, as the sentry at the door seemed to hesitate, he said:

"It is a matter of urgency. I have to see the Colonel as quickly as possible."

It was the way he spoke rather than what he said which convinced the man.

The sentry signalled to another soldier who was listening, and he walked ahead of them.

They moved along passages and up some stairs.

Then the soldier who was leading them knocked on a door.

A voice said:

"Come in," and the man opened it.

The Major walked in first.

A middle-aged man in uniform was sitting at his desk.

He looked up and said:

"I have been watching your progress through the valley towards us and I cannot imagine a more idiotic—"

He stopped suddenly.

The Major had removed the hat he was wearing and his dark glasses.

"Good Lord!" the Colonel exclaimed. "It is you, Wicke. What the hell are you doing here, and got up in that extraordinary manner?"

"It was the only way I could think of to reach you

inconspicuously," the Major replied, "and I have brought with me Miss Lonsdale, who has discovered, as she speaks Russian, that you are to be attacked at Midnight."

The Colonel stared at the Major as if he could not believe what he was hearing.

Then he said:

"Are you sure of this?"

"Absolutely sure," the Major replied. "And a bomb has already been placed on the North-West Rampart to create a breach in the wall."

The Colonel picked up a bell which was lying on his desk and rang it violently.

The door opened.

"All officers are to come here immediately," the Colonel ordered.

The soldier saluted and left the room.

The Colonel looked at Mavina.

"Did you say Miss Lonsdale?" he asked.

"She is Richard Lonsdale's daughter," the Major answered. "She saved our lives last night, which is another story, and most important, she overheard the Russian plans to attack you tonight."

"I find it hard to believe," Colonel Stephenson said, "but naturally I am exceedingly grateful. Please, Miss Lonsdale, sit down while we wait for you to tell my officers exactly what you heard."

Because she felt a little bewildered and overawed by the occasion, Mavina looked at the Major.

It was as if she were waiting for his instructions.

He smiled at her and brought a chair forward which he put beside the Colonel.

Then he fetched one for himself.

"We are very thirsty," he said, "as we have had nothing to eat or drink since breakfast in Peshawar.

All that mattered was to reach you as soon as possible, and I thought it dangerous to stop on the way."

"Very dangerous indeed," the Colonel agreed. "I could not believe it when one of my look-outs told me you were driving towards us through the valley which has been out of bounds for weeks."

He was about to add how many people had been killed, then caught the Major's eyes.

He knew it would be a mistake to upset Mavina.

"It is a surprise, Miss Lonsdale," he said, "to find you here, but at the same time, we are very honoured that you should visit us."

Mavina was just about to explain why she had come, when the door opened.

The officers the Colonel had sent for came hurrying in.

There were fifteen of them, and she gathered that some others were on duty.

They, therefore, could not obey the immediate call from the Colonel.

He waited until the door had shut, then rose to his feet.

"I have just received, gentlemen," he said, "two visitors whom you will certainly know by name. We all have a deep admiration for Major Willoughby Wicke and the magnificent work he has done for us here and in other parts of India."

He paused, and then continued:

"He has brought with him today the daughter of Colonel Richard Lonsdale, whom we all admired and whose death was a tragedy we shall never forget. Miss Lonsdale will now tell you what is planned to happen here tonight."

Because Mavina had been a little bemused at their

arrival, she had not realised that she was expected to speak to the officers.

Now, as the Colonel sat down, she looked at the Major pleadingly.

"Do not bother to stand up," he said. "Just tell them quite simply exactly what you overheard, starting when you saw the man walking towards the Dak bungalow."

The quietness with which he spoke and the fact that he was sitting close to her made it possible for Mavina to do what he asked.

She told herself the only thing that mattered was that they should be prepared for the onslaught.

She raised her voice a little so that the men crowded in the room could hear.

She started by saying how she had been watching the stars and the moonlight and had seen a man approaching the bungalow.

She explained how he had climbed over the balcony and in through a window.

She had thought it was the English artist they had been told was staying in the next room.

Then, when she had gone to wash her hands because she had been holding the curtain which was dirty, she had heard him talking in Russian.

She saw the eyes of the officers who were listening to her widen as she said this.

She told them that she had heard the man say, "We are going to attack the Fort at Midnight."

He had also said that a bomb had been planted in the North-West Rampart which would enable them to take the Fort by surprise and kill everyone in it.

Mavina thought there was no point in adding that he had said that she and the Major would be murdered first.

When she finished, she looked at him for approval, and he smiled at her.

She saw by the expression in his eyes that she had done what he wanted.

Now all the officers seemed to be talking at once.

The Colonel held up his hand.

"The first thing we have to do is to remove the bomb," he said, "or, rather, make it harmless. We must not be seen to be doing so, and if it cannot be found inside the walls, you will have to go outside."

He paused as if he were thinking, then went on:

"You can either drill your men so that what we are doing behind them cannot be seen by those watching us, or else take carts piled with hay or any other commodity to disguise what is happening behind them."

There was a murmur of approval at this, and the Colonel continued:

"If they are attacking us in the North-West, we must be ready for them with guns and men. Choose your positions and make quite certain that you work out exactly how they will approach us."

He turned towards Mavina as he added:

"Thanks to Miss Lonsdale, we know where it will be. It will be where they have laid the bomb to make an entrance for them into the Fort."

The officers nodded to indicate they understood.

The Colonel then looked at the clock.

"We have plenty of time," he said, "to move two of the larger guns, and every man in the Fort is to be on full alert from the moment it grows dark."

The officers left the room, and the Colonel said:

"Now, Wicke, I can offer you and Miss Lonsdale something to eat and drink, and I expect after that she would like to lie down."

Mavina looked pleadingly at the Major, and he said:

"The reason Miss Lonsdale is here is that she has come to India to find her Father's grave."

For a moment the Colonel looked startled, then he said:

"I imagine it is you, Wicke, who discovered where it is."

"It was not very difficult," the Major remarked.

"Of course we will take Miss Lonsdale to see it," Colonel Stephenson said, "as soon as you have had some refreshment."

He took them down to the Dining-Room which was used by the officers.

The servants were told to provide them with anything that was cold and ready.

It was a joy to be able to have a cool drink.

Mavina, at the Major's suggestion, took off her hat and coat.

As both were covered in dust, she felt rather guilty as it fell on the floor when she removed them.

When she had eaten and drunk, she felt the tiredness and dizziness leaving her.

As they finished their meal, she looked at the Major.

He knew without her saying anything what she wanted.

The Colonel led them out of the Fort and into the North Compound.

There were a great number of soldiers moving about, obviously planning their tactics to meet the attack.

The Colonel turned to the West, where the high peak of the mountain towered into the sky.

There was no-one near them, and now the Colonel stopped.

"I think, Miss Lonsdale," he said, "because you have come here with Major Wicke, you are aware that your Father was taking part in the Great Game. Anyone who is a member of it is unknown to anyone else taking part. Yet, because of the brilliance of some outstanding men, it was inevitable they should become known."

"And Papa was . . . one of . . . those," Mavina said, almost beneath her breath.

"Your Father was magnificent," the Colonel said, "and those who knew him not only loved him as a man but admired him because of his achievements where few others would venture."

Mavina clasped her hands together, and the Colonel went on:

"Your Father had gone out on a particularly difficult mission, of course heavily disguised. He came back here riding a tired camel, and as he reached the main gates, a sentry challenged him and he dismounted."

The Colonel's voice deepened as he continued:

"The gate was just being opened to him when a shot from behind the rocks hit your Father in the back. He fell to the ground and was carried inside the Fort. I happened to be in the compound when it happened, and when I reached him I realised who he was."

The Colonel was obviously moved by what he was saying.

"He then looked up at me," he went on," and said: 'In my saddle-bag and you will be pleased with them, John!' Then he shut his eyes and died."

The Colonel's voice almost broke as he finished, and Mavina, listening, struggled to hold back her tears.

She knew it was something her Father would not like.

With an almost superhuman effort she managed to prevent herself from weakening.

"Because it was not possible to reward your Father for what was an outstanding achievement in our campaign against the Russians," the Colonel said, "we buried him here, where I thought he would like to be, and he will never be forgotten."

The Colonel moved forward as he spoke, and Mavina saw against the rampart wall there was a rough piece of ground which had obviously been dug for a grave.

"We are having a tombstone made," he said, "but it is taking a little time. It will carry your Father's name and the date of his death. Every man who comes to this Fort will know he died to save us and India from the Russians."

Mavina clenched her fingers together until they were bloodless, but she still did not cry.

Then, to her surprise, the Major opened a parcel that he was holding in his hand.

She had noticed when they got into the *Tika-Gharri* that besides their suitcase and his leather bag there was a paper parcel.

She had wondered vaguely what it was.

Now the Major opened it and drew out what she saw was a wreath.

It was small but very skillfuly made as only the Indians can make flowers look like jewels.

It was in three colours, red, white, and blue.

Mavina thought as the Major placed it in her hands it was just like him to have thought of something so appropriate.

She went down on her knees and placed the wreath

on the top of the grave where she thought her Father's head would be.

Then she looked up at the mountain peak far above them which was golden in the afternoon sun.

The Major knew she was not only praying but speaking to her Father.

She believed he had brought her there safely despite all the difficulties.

Then, when she rose to her feet, they walked back in silence to the main building.

Then the Major insisted that Mavina was given a Bedroom so that she could rest.

"I am sure," he said, "you do not want to sit about talking, and anyway, there is no-one to talk to. Everyone has a job to do and it would be a great mistake to distract them even for a few minutes."

"Of course," Mavina agreed.

The Bedroom was small, and she thought that it had not been used very often.

If it was a guest-room, that was not surprising.

She was certain that no-one would want to visit the Fort unless they were absolutely obliged to do so.

She lay down on the bed, but she could not sleep.

She was thinking about what would happen tonight and hoping that nothing would go wrong.

"I am sure, Papa," she said to her Father, "it was you who brought me here and made the Major take us to that Dak bungalow where I overheard the Russian. Now it is you who will save the Fort, so please do not let . . . anyone be . . . killed."

She saw later, when the Major came to speak to her, that he had changed into his uniform which he must have brought with him in the suitcase.

This meant he intended to take part in the fighting.

She wanted to beg him not to do anything stupid or to go into danger.

It was not his battle!

Surely the garrison of the Fort could manage without him.

Yet she knew instinctively he would not listen to her.

He would perhaps despise her for being frightened when her Father had done so much without fear and without thought of himself for the country he loved.

"Now, you are to stay here when the attack starts," the Major was saying. "You must promise me that you will not come out under any circumstances."

"Must . . . I stay . . . alone?" Mavina said.

The words seemed to come to her lips without her really thinking about them.

She knew the answer before the Major said:

"You know I have to do my part in defeating a ruthless enemy who has no right to invade our country."

Mavina did not answer, and after a moment he added:

"I think you know what your Father would expect of you and me."

"Yes . . . I . . . know," Mavina murmured.

"You were very brave today," the Major said, "and I am sure he was extremely proud of you."

"It was very . . . kind of . . . you to bring . . . a wreath," Mavina murmured. "I did . . . not think . . . of it."

"I think your contribution to all this cannot be expressed by words or flowers," the Major replied.

He put his hand on her shoulder.

"Just pray," he said, "as you prayed before, that

things will go right, and I am sure your prayers will be heard."

He went from the room before she could think of an answer.

The servant brought her something to eat and drink, but she felt the food would choke her.

Then, as the hands of the clock moved slowly, she knew that the enemy was approaching.

They would be supremely confident that they would take the Fort by surprise.

She wished now she had asked the Major if they had managed to find the bomb and render it harmless.

Then, as the hands of the clock touched twelve, there was a single shot.

She thought it might be a small gun which was to set off the bomb.

There was one shot and then another, followed by a fusillade of shots.

Then there was the noise of a large gun firing, again and again.

She knew that this was a reply from the Fort.

Because the noise was almost deafening, she put her hands up over her ears.

It seemed to Mavina as if the firing went on interminably.

Actually it could not have been longer than twenty minutes.

The whole Fort seemed to be shaking from the gunfire.

But she knew it was the guns inside that were causing the noise and not those on the attack.

Yet there was some cross-fire, until suddenly, almost eerily, there was silence.

The silence seemed even more frightening than the noise.

'Suppose,' Mavina thought, 'everyone has been killed? Suppose the attackers are even now entering through the ramparts to finish off those they have not yet destroyed?'

If everybody was killed, was the Major killed too?

She felt, whatever he had said, she must find out the truth, and rose from the bed on which she was sitting.

Even as she did so, the door opened and the Major came in.

She looked at him and then she gave a little cry.

"You . . . are . . . safe! You . . . are . . . safe!"

She ran towards him as if she must touch him to make certain he was really there and not just an illusion.

"We are all safe, thanks to you," the Major said.

She was looking up at him, her eyes searching his to make sure he was telling her the truth.

"We are all very grateful, Mavina," he said gently, and his lips touched hers.

For a moment she could not believe it was happening.

Then, as she felt a streak of sunshine run through her body, there were footsteps outside the door.

A moment later Colonel Stephenson came into the room.

"We have just achieved a notable victory, Miss Lonsdale," he said, "and I do not know how I can begin to thank you."

Mavina had moved from the Major's arms, and the Colonel said:

"Come to my room. I feel we must celebrate this

memorable occasion, and quite frankly I need a drink."

The Major laughed.

"And so do I. I can hardly believe it would go off so well, I must specially congratulate your men on finding the bomb and dismantling it so effectively."

"Without our enemies being aware of it," the Colonel added.

They reached the Colonel's private Sitting-Room, and a servant brought in a bottle of Champagne.

When it was poured out, the Colonel raised his glass to Mavina.

"I can only thank you from the bottom of my heart," he said, "for saving the Fort and my men. I know your Father would have been very proud of you."

"Since it is due to my Father that I am here," Mavina said, "and also because he insisted that I learned Russian, I think, Colonel, the victory is really his."

"Just another that he has achieved for India," the Colonel murmured. "He was a great man and we should never have lost him."

It was the Major who explained to Mavina how surprised the enemy must have been, first of all, when their bomb did not explode as they had expected.

Secondly, the guns which ploughed into them were not what they expected on that side of the Fort.

It was after two o'clock in the morning when the Colonel learned that the British soldiers had found a hundred and twenty-nine tribesmen dead near the Fort.

There would be others further away, and undoubtedly a number of wounded.

Well enough to retreat from the gunfire, many of them had left their weapons behind.

The Colonel was delighted, and so were the other officers who had reported to him.

It was three o'clock when the Major said that he thought Mavina should rest, as he wished to leave early next morning.

He hoped on this occasion they would be escorted to Peshawar, as he did not wish to make the journey again in anything so uncomfortable as the *Tika-Gharri*.

"You shall have every cushion and pillow there is in the Fort," the Colonel said as he laughed.

Finally Mavina was persuaded to go to the Bedroom she had occupied before.

When she said goodnight to the Major, he merely pressed her hand and said:

"Try to sleep. We have a journey in front of us tomorrow which you will find quite tiring."

It was only when she was in bed that she thought of his words.

He was sending her back to Calcutta.

'He has done what he promised,' she thought, 'and now there is no need for him to bother with me anymore.'

He had kissed her and she knew it was the most wonderful thing that had ever happened.

It had given her a rapture she did not even know existed.

To him, however, it was just an expression of gratitude and he would never think of it again.

She tossed and turned on the comfortable little bed which was very different from what she had slept on last night.

Suddenly she realised she was in love.

She loved the Major, which was just as practical as loving the moon.

He was as out of reach as the stars she had looked

130

at from the Dak bungalow.

It was her wanting to see them which had saved not only his life and her own but the Fort for which her Father had died.

So much had happened, things which seemed overwhelming in their intensity.

Yet now there was nothing for her to do but to go back to England.

She had come to India to find her Father's grave.

She had found it because she had been fortunate enough to meet the Major, and he had been kind to her.

No man could have done more.

No man except him would have been brave enough to bring her to the Fort and to have thought of bringing a wreath.

After what had been said when they had been drinking the Champagne, she realised that it was only by a miracle she and the Major had not been shot down as they drove towards the Fort.

The previous week twelve people had lost their lives.

Before that there had been many other unaccounted-for deaths.

'The Major risked his life to bring me here,' Mavina thought, 'and no-one could have been kinder, no-one more considerate. Now I must go out of his life the same way I came into it.'

She knew that to love him would be an agony beyond words, the same agony she had felt when she saw him dancing with Lady Flora, but now far more intense.

"I love . . . him . . . I love . . . him," she whispered in the darkness.

But there was no prayer to go with it, no pleading

that he would love her in return.

She knew the answer only too well.

He had befriended her because he admired her Father.

He had done everything he could, which was very much more than most men would have done, to show his admiration for a man who died in the Great Game.

He would have no wish to encumber himself with a tiresome young woman who clung to him because she was frightened.

She had no part in the social world of the Viceroy and the beautiful women in which the Major moved.

She remembered how she had decided she would find a job in India, teaching children.

She knew now that India was too big and she would be frightened alone, frightened of the men who would pursue her like the man on the ship or the elderly man who had tried to kiss her.

Now she knew what a kiss meant.

Now she had felt the rapture that had swept through her body when the Major's lips had touched her.

She could never let another man come near her.

'I love . . . him,' she thought miserably, 'and when I am . . . gone he will . . . never think of me . . . again.'

Then the tears came, tears she had held back so bravely.

Tears which were not for the past, but for the future.

chapter seven

The following morning they certainly set off in very different style from how they had arrived.

Because Mavina had hardly slept all night and was exhausted from weeping, she was very quiet.

The Major was in high spirits.

After daylight the count of the enemy who had been killed was over two hundred.

The Colonel was quite convinced it would be a long time before they struck again.

But he was taking no risks.

An open carriage drawn by two horses was provided for Mavina and the Major.

There were two soldiers riding on either side of it.

Behind them came a big Army brake containing twenty soldiers, all fully armed.

It was a sunny morning but not too hot when they set out.

The Major was, of course, wearing his uniform, and Mavina thought how handsome and smart he looked.

At the same time, she felt that every mile they traversed was taking her to Calcutta.

This was the preliminary stage of her return to England.

They passed without any incident through the twisting, stony valley which led up to the Fort.

Much more speedily than on their outward journey, they reached the streams, the trees, and the dust.

There were camels like those Mavina had seen before, Rickshaws, and *Tika-Gharris* carrying people into Peshawar to do their shopping.

They were back in civilisation!

When they reached the Station it was, as usual crowded with people of every type and class as well as children, Priests, and goats, besides a number of soldiers who saluted them when they appeared.

The Major sent a message to the adjacent Hotel to tell Hill that he was wanted.

As if he were clairvoyant, he was in fact waiting just inside the Station with their luggage beside him.

"I thinks as how you would be turning up this morning, Sir," he said to the Major.

An officer who was with them went to arrange about their accommodation on the train.

Mavina saw him talking with the Stationmaster.

She felt sure they would be as comfortable as they were when they left Calcutta.

She was not mistaken.

The officer came back and said that the first coach, which was always the best, had been allotted to them.

Someone of less importance who had booked it had been moved further down the train.

It was exactly the same as the one they had had before.

The comfortable Drawing-Room, two Bedrooms, a Pantry, and a bed for Hill next door were all waiting for them.

The officers who had come with them, and there were four of them, inspected it.

Then they stood on the platform just outside, talking to the Major about what had happened last night.

Mavina was silent.

She did not want to remember how frightened she had been when the guns were pounding.

She had been so desperately afraid that the Major might be injured.

She was looking at the people who were now beginning to board the train.

She noticed a man come onto the platform in a great hurry.

He had a square head on wide shoulders.

Because there was a pile of someone's luggage in his way, he flung his left leg over it.

He used his left rather than his right leg, and suddenly Mavina knew who he was.

She put her hand on the arm of the Major, who was standing beside her.

"That man . . . there," she said in a whisper, "is the . . . Russian who . . . told the artist . . . to kill us."

Her voice was almost incoherent, but the Major heard her.

Without asking questions, he said sharply to the two officers standing beside him:

"Arrest that man!"

He pointed him out as he spoke.

The Russian had by this time reached a carriage a little way down the platform.

The two officers ran towards him, followed by the Major.

The other two, who had not heard what he said, were therefore not certain what was happening.

Just as the officers reached the Russian, he looked round and realised they were approaching him.

He put his hand into his pocket and pulled out a revolver.

He raised it, intending to shoot the first officer approaching him.

With a swiftness which came from long training, the officer struck his arm upwards as he pulled the trigger.

There was a resounding bang, and a bullet went up towards the roof.

Just for a second there was silence, then several women screamed.

The soldiers who had escorted them in the brake came running from the back of the platform.

They had been waiting to cheer the Major and Mavina when the train left.

The Russian was struggling with the two officers who had first approached him.

They had him in control by the time the soldiers joined them.

"Tie him up!" the Major ordered. "And charge him first with causing the death of a Russian disguised as an English artist who was murdered in the Dak bungalow the night before last. Afterwards he is to be interrogated about what happened at the Fort last night."

It was then the Russian cursed him speaking a mixture of English, Urdu, and Russian.

The soldiers took him away while the travellers on the platform stared as he passed them.

The Major walked back to his own coach.

Mavina had not moved, she had only watched, looking pale and frightened.

"That was very clever of you," the Major said quietly.

It was then the Stationmaster was at his side, saying:

"Have I your permission, Major *Sahib*, to start the train? Already it is two minutes late."

"You have my permission, Stationmaster," the Major replied.

He shook hands with the officers and thanked them.

Then, as he stepped into the coach, the engine began puffing and blowing until it started to move very slowly.

The officer saluted, and so did the soldiers who had not left with the prisoner.

Then, as the train quickened its pace, they cheered and waved their caps.

When they were out of sight, the Major turned from the window and realised how pale Mavina was looking.

"It has been too much for you," he said, "at the same time, you have once again struck a blow against the enemy which may have far-reaching results. I have the feeling that particular Russian was of importance, and it is due to him there has been so much disturbance recently round the fort."

"I am . . . glad that I . . . recognised . . . him," Mavina said faintly.

"It was extremely clever of you," the Major said, "especially as you told me that you had not been able to see his face as he approached the bungalow."

"He was silhouetted against the . . . moonlight,"

Mavina said, "and it was his square head and wide shoulders I . . . noticed. Although I did not . . . think of it until . . . just now, he climbed using his . . . left leg first while most people use their . . . right."

"As I have already said, it was extremely clever of you," the Major said. "That is exactly the sort of detail we are taught to notice in the Great Game."

He smiled as he spoke.

Then Hill, who had just come into the Drawing-Room, said:

"Your luncheon's ready, Sir, and the officers left you a bottle of Champagne with the Colonel's compliments."

"That was kind of him," the Major said, "and I think, Mavina, after that long drive, we both need it!"

She sat down at the table.

Hill waited on them and poured out the Champagne.

But all she could think of was the train gathering speed towards Calcutta.

Soon she would be taking leave of the Major.

She looked at him on the other side of the table.

She thought no other man could look so handsome or, at the moment, so pleased with life.

She knew it was because they had won the battle last night.

She had also found the Russian who was at the bottom of all the trouble.

'That is what interests him,' she told herself, 'the Great Game! A duel with the enemy, pitting his brain against theirs.'

She had been very touched when before they left the Fort, the Colonel said to her:

"You know, Miss Lonsdale, there are no words with which I can express my gratitude and that of my men. You saved us last night not only from a humiliating defeat and the loss of many lives, but also from a blow against British supremacy in India which, as your Father knew, is absolutely vital."

He paused before he went on:

"I am sure you are aware that the Russians are trying to infiltrate the country and eventually drive us out."

Mavina made a little murmur, as she did know this, and he continued:

"It is something which must never happen, and it is men like your Father and Major Wicke who will prevent it."

He smiled at her and then added:

"And of course, women like yourself, who were sent not only to help us but to inspire us, which is exactly, Miss Lonsdale, what you have done."

Mavina thanked him.

He promised to send her a photograph of her Father's grave as soon as the tombstone was erected.

Then, when she and the Major drove off, the soldiers who were left behind at the Fort first saluted them, then cheered them.

Their voices rang out, and Mavina could still hear them as the carriage drove down the twisting road into the valley.

Now she realised it was all over.

When the Major left her, she would no longer be a heroine, just an unimportant English girl who could not possibly stay alone in India with no money to support her.

'I . . . will have to . . . go . . . home,' she thought for the hundredth time since she had cried last night.

But there was no home waiting for her in England. She was frightened of the voyage back, in case there was another man to pursue her as she had been pursued as soon as she left Tilbury.

There would be no Major to turn to, because there could never be another man like him.

"You are very silent," the Major said, "but of course you are tired. We were very late going to bed last night and had practically no sleep the night before."

Mavina put down her knife and fork.

"I . . . am not . . . hungry," she said. "Perhaps . . . if I . . . rested for a . . . little while I . . . would feel . . . better."

"That would certainly be the sensible thing to do," the Major said, "and I can tell you it is what I intend to do myself."

He smiled at her, but she did not smile back.

She was rising a little unsteadily from the table.

The Major looked at Hill, who hurried to open the door of her Bedroom.

He had already undone one of the trunks while they had been talking to the officers.

Mavina saw there was one of her Mother's pretty nightgowns lying on the bed.

Without asking her permission, Hill unbuttoned her dress at the back.

He then went from the compartment.

With an effort, because she really did feel dizzy and faint, Mavina pulled off her clothes.

She threw them down on the floor which was something she never did normally.

Then she put on her nightgown, loosened her hair, and got into bed.

Almost as soon as her head touched the pillow, she fell asleep.

It was the deep sleep of exhaustion.

She had no idea that Hill came back quietly into the

room, picked up her clothes, and tidied them away.

She did not know that the Major looked in at her, not once, but several times.

Later that night he stood for quite a long time looking at her as she slept.

The train rushed on and on.

Mavina was lost to the world—a world that although she did not know it, she had not seen before.

She came back to consciousness aware first of the train-wheels turning over beneath her.

She thought vaguely that she must get up and have dinner with the Major.

She suddenly felt more like herself.

While she was still a little sleepy, she no longer felt dizzy or faint.

Then the door opened and Hill put his head round it.

He saw her eyes were open, and exclaimed:

"You're awake, Miss, that's good! We'll be arriving in another twenty minutes and th' Major thinks you should get dressed."

"What is the time?" Mavina asked.

"Ten o'clock in th' morning, Miss," Hill said. "You've slept all afternoon and all night, not a peep or a squeak out o' you."

He grinned at the astonishment on her face, then added:

"I've put your clothes, Miss, ready for you, and 't would be a mistake to keep th' Major waiting."

Mavina knew this was true.

When Hill disappeared, she jumped out of bed and went to the window.

Then she could only stare in astonishment.

There were mountains, huge mountains, all round them and stretching away into the distance.

The highest of them was snow-capped.

She knew they were the Himalayas.

Bewildered, she wondered why they were not going straight to Calcutta as she expected.

Then she remembered it was April, when the Viceroy and Vicereine moved to Simla.

So that is where we are, and her heart sank.

The Major was going to Simla because first he would be with the Viceroy and secondly Lady Flora would be there.

She felt a sharp pain in her breast which was like a dagger stabbing her.

She remembered how beautiful Lady Flora was and how she had looked at the Major when they were dancing in the Ballroom.

"Simla! He will certainly not want me there," Mavina told herself.

She dressed quickly because she did not want to annoy him.

She arranged her hair in the way she had always done it.

At least his last memories of her would not be of the plain woman she had been as the Doctor's wife.

The adventure was over!

The adventure when they had been together, when they fought the Russians side by side.

The Major had already fulfilled his promise to take her to find her Father's grave.

He had done it at a considerable risk to himself.

Mavina shuddered to think how easily he might have been killed by the Russian disguised as an artist.

Then he had insisted on fighting at the Fort because it would be expected of him.

She had perhaps also saved him from the Russian who was boarding their train at Peshawar.

When she went back to England, he would continue to be in danger, but she would not be there to save him.

The train was slowing down, and she hurriedly went into the Drawing-Room.

The Major rose from the table when she came in.

"Good morning, Miss Rip Van Winkle," he said. "I was beginning to think I would have to carry you off the train in your nightgown."

"I am sorry," Mavina said, "I was so tired, I do not think I moved all night."

"I can confirm that," the Major said, "and it was the best thing you could possibly do. Now, drink some coffee which is waiting for you, and if you are hungry, there will be a meal as soon as we arrive."

At least, Mavina thought, he was taking her to Simla with him!

He was not making her travel on alone.

She quickly drank the coffee and ate a small piece of toast and marmalade.

Then the train was puffing noisily into the Station.

When they got out, there were servants in what Mavina thought was a very smart uniform.

Simla was smaller than she had somehow expected it to be.

There was a carriage waiting for them outside, and the Viceroy was certainly welcoming the Major very handsomely.

Drawn by four horses, the carriage was very smart.

There was an escort of six soldiers on horse-back riding ahead and behind them.

It was, however, impossible to look at anything but the mountains towering above.

The trees in the valley where the Station was situated were covered not only with the leaves of spring but with pink and white blossoms.

It was incredibly beautiful.

Then, as they started to climb up what was a very steep hill, Mavina felt they were climbing the mountains themselves.

She found it strange that there seemed very few houses or buildings after they had left the Railway Station.

She had never been to Simla.

Someone, however, had told her that it was very difficult for the Viceroy to be private.

Whenever he ventured out of Government House in Calcutta, he could be seen by numbers of people.

There certainly seemed no-one to notice them here, and Mavina thought perhaps it was because they had a long way to go.

Then, as they climbed higher and higher, she saw in front of her a large house not unlike a Scottish Castle.

It was not quite like the descriptions she had heard of the Viceregal Lodge in Simla.

It was a two-storeyed mansion with a row of battlemented turrets, some square, others octagonal, and a Gothic *porte-cochere* and verandahs.

There were creepers climbing up the stone-work, and the house was such a surprise that she could only stare at it.

The carriage drew to a standstill outside the front-door which had large Gothic arches leading into a hall.

A number of servants in white, scarlet, and gold appeared bowing politely.

An officer, who Mavina assumed was an aide-de-camp, stepped forward to say:

"It is a great honour to welcome you here, my Lord.

I hope you had a good journey."

"Very good, thank you," the Major replied, "but Miss Lonsdale and I are both extremely hungry and we would like something to eat and drink as soon as possible."

"It is ready for you, my Lord," the A.D.C. said. "If you would come this way."

Mavina thought it was strange for him to address the Major as "my Lord."

Then the Major spoke to one of the servants who addressed him as "Lord *Sahib*," so she supposed that was what was correct here, if nowhere else.

They were shown into a large Dining-Room.

As they entered, there were *Khitmagars*, wearing the same white, scarlet, and gold uniforms.

They were drawn up in a line and saluted them.

Mavina was to learn later that this was the custom in the Government Houses of the North-West, where they were more ceremonial than in any other Government Houses.

At this moment, however, she was more concerned with the table on which lay their breakfast.

It was covered with a damask cloth, and the napkins were cunningly folded to resemble exotic birds.

At the Major's suggestion, she took off her hat and put it on a chair.

She also removed the short coat she had worn over her dress when she left the train.

"If you are not hungry," the Major said, "then you ought to be, and I think you will find the food here is a great improvement on what we have been obliged to eat since we left Calcutta."

"You have . . . not told me . . . where we are," Mavina said. "I thought when I . . . saw the Himalayas we must be . . . going to Simla."

"Is that where you wanted to go?" the Major enquired.

Mavina shook her head.

"No! No! I think...I should...hate Simla. This seems...quiet and very...lovely."

She wanted to say, 'I can be alone with you.'

But she thought if she did it might frighten the Major into sending her away even more quickly than he intended to do.

'Perhaps we are only staying one night,' she thought, 'and tomorrow we shall be on our way again.'

The food they were served by the *Khitmagars* was delicious.

Mavina suddenly found that she was extremely hungry.

The iced drinks they were given had an exquisite flavour.

The meal did not take long, then the Major, rising to his feet, said:

"I am going first to show you the flowers, which are different here from any other place in the whole of India."

They walked out of the Dining-Room.

They had reached the front-door when the A.D.C. appeared holding what Mavina saw was a number of letters in his hand.

Her heart sank.

"I think one of these is rather urgent, My Lord," the A.D.C. said.

The Major hesitated.

Then, as if he felt business must come first, he said to Mavina:

"If you go on out of the house and turn left, I will join you in a few minutes."

146

She did as she was told.

Then she was suddenly aware that the garden on that side of the house was fragrant and breathtakingly beautiful with lilies-of-the valley.

Beyond them the slopes were scarlet with rhododendrons.

They were so beautiful that Mavina could only stand staring at what she was seeing.

'It might be a dream rather than reality,' she thought.

Then she was aware that the grass was intensely green.

The tree-trunks were covered with moss.

The ferns gave an exotic touch to the English oaks, beeches, and chestnuts which had been planted there.

Fascinated, she moved forward across the lawn.

In the paths on either side of it there were mauve orchids just coming into bud.

White clematis covered the jungle-shrubs.

"It just cannot be true!" she said aloud.

"It is too . . . too . . . beautiful."

She walked on as if in a dream.

Then suddenly the trees parted and there were the mountains climbing one above the other.

High against the sky she could see the white snow glistening in the sunshine.

She stared at them, transfixed, until she heard someone behind her.

She knew who it was, and her heart turned a somersault.

"I thought I would find you here," the Major said in a deep voice. "It is my favourite place. Five years ago there was a landslide which buried houses and the Assembly Rooms in the valley."

"Why did . . . that . . . happen?" Mavina asked.

The Major smiled.

"According to local legends, the lake down below grew out of a hole dug by the Goddess Naini."

Mavina gave a little gasp.

"I have heard of her."

"Then you know where you are," the Major said. "This is the hill station of Naini Tal, Summer Capital of the North-West Provinces."

"I never thought of our being here," Mavina murmured.

"So you understand the landslide was a revenge of the Goddess who had forbidden this place to strangers," the Major said. "But I assure you, we are now twelve hundred feet above the lake and perfectly safe."

He spoke in a very re-assuring voice.

Then he said quietly:

"I have something to tell you."

Mavina thought he was going to explain why he must send her away.

She could not stay alone with him in this enchanted place.

"I have discovered," the Major went on, "what happened to your Father's money."

This was not what Mavina had expected him to say, and she turned to look at him but did not speak.

"Your Father lent everything he possessed," the Major went on, "to a Chinese man who wanted to buy more ships, and who could not himself raise the money for them at that particular moment."

He paused and then continued:

"He was extremely grateful to your Father for helping him, and the money he invested with him has trebled in value. At any time you wish, the Chinese man will give you about thirty thousand pounds. If you leave it with him, it will increase year by year."

"That was . . . clever of . . . Papa," Mavina said.

"Of course it was, like everything else he did," the Major agreed. "So now you know, Mavina, that if you want, you can employ a Chaperon to take you round India which you thought you could not afford, or an elderly Courier."

Mavina drew in her breath.

He had said it, it had come, those were her marching orders.

If she behaved correctly, she should thank him for all he had done for her and accept his suggestion of an elderly Courier.

Then she knew she could not stay in India and be unable to see the Major.

It was something which would tear her apart!

How could she be in the same country but be separated from him?

"I have another proposition to make," the Major said after what seemed a long silence. "It is that you might prefer to stay with me."

Mavina thought at first she could not have heard him correctly.

Then she turned round, her eyes very wide and questioning, to look at him.

"Did . . . you . . . say," she asked in a voice which did not sound like her own, "that I . . . could stay . . . with . . . you?"

The light that had been missing from her eyes ever since she woke was shining again.

The Major looked at her searchingly before he said:

"Yes, if that would make you happy. But as I must be careful of my reputation, I think we should be married."

149

He saw Mavina's face transformed with a radiance which made her more beautiful than any woman he had ever seen.

Then, as if she still thought she was misunderstanding what he had said, she asked:

"You ... really mean ... that I should be ... your wife?"

The Major smiled.

"I think, my Darling," he said, "you cannot do without me, and I am quite certain I cannot do without you."

"It ... cannot ... be ... true," Mavina whispered.

"The only question that is worrying me," the Major went on, "is whether you love me enough. I know you are frightened of men and I have no wish for you to be frightened of me."

"I ... love ... you ... I ... love ... you," Mavina said, "and I ... have never been ... frightened of ... you."

"I thought perhaps that was true last night when I kissed you," the Major said. "But we were interrupted, and now I want to be quite certain that you are not afraid."

His arms went round her as he spoke, and his lips were on hers.

To Mavina, it was the ecstasy she had felt before, only far more intense and far more wonderful.

The Major kissed her very gently as if at first he was afraid of frightening her.

He felt the sweetness and innocence of her lips, and at the same time he was aware her body seemed to melt into his.

The little tremor which ran through her was not one of fear.

His kisses became more passionate, more demanding.

Mavina felt they were part of the lilies-of-the-valley, the snow on the mountains, and the sun shining above them.

This was what she had wanted, what she had longed for but thought she would never have!

Only when the Major raised his head did she say:

"It . . . cannot be . . . true . . . I am . . . dreaming."

She clung to him as if she were suddenly afraid she would wake up and find herself in the train.

There would be no Naini Tal, only the emptiness of her small compartment.

"If you are dreaming," the Major said, and his voice was deep and understanding, "then I am dreaming too."

"We will . . . be . . . together," Mavina asked.

He knew the importance of the question, and said:

"Let me explain, my Darling, that I have work to do here different from what I have ever done before."

"It is . . . not . . . dangerous . . . you are not going . . . into danger?" Mavina cried. "I have been thinking of how you . . . might have . . . died in the . . . Dak bungalow or . . . last night when you were . . . fighting the . . . tribesmen or again . . . today if that . . . Russian had come on . . . the train . . . with us."

The terror was back in her eyes, and the Major said quickly:

"No, no, it is nothing like that. This is the Governor's Lodge in what I have just told you is the Summer hill-station of the North-West Provinces. The Governor-General, who is a friend of mine, unfortunately had to go back to England on urgent family affairs and will not be returning to India."

Mavina was listening to him, looking up into his

eyes and still not understanding.

"The Viceroy has therefore asked me," the Major went on, "to become the Governor of the North-West Provinces. I can imagine no-one would be able to help me in what is quite a difficult task as well as you."

"But I am . . . not . . . important . . . enough," Mavina demurred. "You know . . . I have only . . . lived very . . . quietly in . . . the country with Papa and Mama. You need someone who . . . understands your . . . world of Viceroys and . . . great parties."

She was thinking of Lady Flora as she spoke.

She was losing something so precious that without it she had no wish to live.

The Major merely smiled and drew her a little closer.

"I think, my Darling One," he said, "if the Marchioness of Dufferin can make herself the perfect wife for the Viceroy, you, with your beauty, your brilliant brain, and I hope your love, can make a perfect wife for the Governor of the North-West Provinces."

There was just a hint of amusement as he said the last words, but Mavina said seriously:

"You are . . . quite . . . quite certain I can do . . . that? I love—and adore you and I would . . . give my . . . life willingly . . . to save you from being . . . hurt or . . . wounded. But if I hampered . . . your career, it . . . would break . . . my heart."

"My Precious, my Darling," the Major exclaimed, "that is exactly how I want my wife to feel. The one thing I am absolutely sure of is that no other Governor-General, or Viceroy, for that matter, will have such a beautiful wife or one who is so perfect in every way."

Mavina could not answer, because he was kissing

her, kissing her demandingly and fiercely, as if he were afraid someone would take her away from him.

When he lifted his head to look at her, he thought she was even more beautiful than she had been before.

It was like the beauty of the Goddess Naini and the flowers which surrounded them.

"What I have already done," he said, "is to send a message to the Vicar of the Church in the valley to ask him to come to the Lodge tonight and marry us after dinner."

"Tonight?" Mavina murmured.

"That will give you a little time," he said, "to consider what you will wear, and for me to have the Chapel decorated with lilies-of-the-valley."

He looked round at them as he spoke and said:

"Nothing could be a better symbol of you, my Precious One."

Mavina hid her face against his shoulder.

She felt it was still too much for her to realise.

Having thought she had lost the Major for ever, she was actually to become his wife.

As if he understood what she was feeling, he said:

"We have been through so much together, and there is so much more for us to do. As we both love India, we will make sure that your Father did not die in vain."

"You do not . . . think we will . . . be at war . . . with Russia?" Mavina asked.

"I am quire certain at this moment that the Viceroy, with his brilliant diplomatic skill, has managed to avert that. At the same time, the Russians will go on attempting to infiltrate this country, and that is what we have to prevent."

"But you . . . will not . . . be playing . . . any more

part . . . in the Great Game?" Mavina pleaded. "I am afraid . . . desperately . . . afraid it might . . . kill you . . . in the end as . . . it killed Papa."

"I can re-assure you on that if nothing else," the Major said. "There will be no more secret missions for the Lieutenant Governor-General or the North-West Provinces. In fact, my Precious One, you may find it rather dull after the drama of what we have just been through."

He was teasing her, but Mavina said:

"What I . . . want is . . . for you . . . to be . . . safe."

"Which I will try to be for your sake," the Major replied.

He kissed her again, then they walked back slowly towards the house.

She knew there must be a lot of work waiting for him.

She must start by trying not to interefere too much with what he had to do.

She wanted, however, to stay in the garden amongst the flowers.

Just by their beauty they expressed her love.

When the front-door came into sight, she saw the A.D.C. waiting for them, and knew she must be tactful.

"I will go and see about my unpacking," she said as she reached the door.

"I will send a servant to let you know as soon as I am free," the Major answered.

He walked in one direction and Mavina in the other.

She went up the stairs and into the beautiful room that was to be her Bedroom.

There was a large bed in an alcove and there were flowers on the dressing-table.

From the windows she could see the tops of the trees in the garden and beyond them the Himalayas.

There were three maids unpacking her trunks.

Mavina hesitated for a moment, then said:

"I want your help. I am to be married this evening to the Lord *Sahib*, and I do not know what I can wear. As you will understand, I want to look beautiful in this beautiful place."

The Indian woman jumped up in excitement.

"Married! The Lady *Sahib* is to be married!"

They chattered amongst themselves in Urdu, and it was like the noise of small cockatoos.

Suddenly they flung up their arms and gave a cry as if they simultaneously had an idea, and ran from the Bedroom.

Mavina wondered what they were going to show her.

In the meantime she went to the wardrobe where they had hung some of her clothes.

She thought that somehow even her Mother's pretty gowns looked dull.

She wanted her wedding to be something the Major would always remember.

To her it would be the most miraculous thing that had ever happened.

But she was a woman, and as a woman she wanted to look more beautiful for him than any other woman he had ever seen.

Most of all, she wanted to be different.

'How can I be different,' she asked.

The elegant but nevertheless ordinary English gowns she had brought with her would not do.

Then the Indian girls came running back.

As they entered the room, Mavina saw that each one of them had her arms full of saris.

They spread them out on the floor in their brilliant colours, red, blue, green, yellow.

There were, of course, no white ones, because white in India is worn only by widows.

Mavina was very touched to see that some of the saris had never been worn.

They must have been kept for some special occasion, perhaps for their own wedding.

They all talked at once as they explained to her how she would look in the different colours.

Then there was one which, the moment Mavina saw it, she knew was the sari she wanted.

It was a very pale pink, exquisitely embroidered.

As she picked it up, she knew from the sound the Indian girls made that they agreed it was exactly what she should wear.

Then one of them ran down to find the gardener, while another went away to come back with her jewel box.

A message came from the Major that dinner was to take place at seven o'clock and the Priest was arriving just before eight.

He did not ask to see her, and Mavina understood that there was a great deal for him to arrange and an enormous number of orders to be given now that he was in charge.

She had a bath and then the Indian girls dressed her in the pink sari.

As soon as she put it on, she knew it was exactly the way she wanted the Major to see her.

It showed the slimness of her waist, the elegance of her hips, and the soft outline of her breasts.

The gardeners had sent in flowers, small roses which were exactly the pink of the sari, and a profusion of lilies-of-the-valley.

One girl with her delicate fingers made a wreath that might have come straight out of a jeweller's shop.

The flowers were exquisitely blended together.

On Mavina's golden hair it made her look, as they all said, like one of the Goddesses they had worshipped ever since they had left the cradle.

There were Indian bracelets for her small wrists such as no woman in India could be without.

There were also bracelets round her ankles.

Finally she was ready.

When she looked at herself in the mirror, she knew, without being conceited, that she had never looked more lovely.

A servant was bowing in the doorway.

"Lord *Sahib* waiting for Lady *Sahib* in hall."

Shyly Mavina went downstairs.

Now, at the last moment, she was afraid in case he would have preferred her as an English bride with a veil over her face.

He was in the hall, magnificent, she thought, in the evening-dress of a Governor-General.

There were orders shining on his coat which she did not know he had received.

But as she approached him, she was looking into his eyes for him to approve or disapprove.

For a moment she held her breath.

Then he said in a very deep voice:

"You are just as I wanted you to look, and even more beautiful and more lovely."

She slipped her arm into his, and they went into dinner.

Once again the *Khitmagar*s were saluting them, and now she understood it was because their Lord *Sahib* was so important and they were exceedingly proud to have him there.

She could not remember afterwards what she had eaten at dinner, although she knew it was delicious.

She was aware only that every time her eyes met those of the man opposite her, their voices died away.

They forgot what they were saying.

There was Champagne to drink, but Mavina was so excited, so thrilled at what was happening, that there was no need for any stimulant.

As dinner finished, a servant announced that the Vicar had arrived and was in the Chapel.

The Major rose and held out his arm.

Mavina moved closer to him, and they walked slowly along the passage which led to the Chapel.

It was only a small one which had been added after the house had been built.

On Sundays the Governor-General went down into what was called the village where the Church which had been destroyed by the land-slide had been re-built.

While Mavina was choosing her wedding-gown upstairs, the gardeners had been busy.

The Chapel was a bower of flowers, mostly lilies-of-the-valley, but with some large Madonna lilies as well.

The scent of them was almost overpowering, but Mavina could not imagine any wedding could be more lovely.

The Priest was an elderly man with white hair.

He read the service with deep sincerity.

When he blessed them, Mavina felt that she and her husband were enveloped with a light that was not of this world but came from Heaven itself.

The A.D.C. was the only witness present.

When the bride and groom left the Chapel, it was he who was ordered to entertain the Priest.

They went straight upstairs to their Bedroom.

When they reached it, Mavina saw that while they had been at dinner, the girls and the gardeners had been busy again.

There were flowers everywhere!

Not white flowers like those in the Chapel, but pink, red, and scarlet rhododendrons.

There were roses which were the colour of her sari, and a great number of exotic flowers of which she did not know the name.

Once again it was a fairy story, a dream that had nothing to do with reality.

She looked at the Major, and he said very gently:

"I think, my Darling, you must allow me to get out of my finery before I tell you how beautiful you are."

She smiled at him, but he did not kiss her.

He merely looked at her for a long moment and then went from the room.

She took off the sari and her wreath, and put on her nightgown which was lying waiting for her on the bed.

She could not resist going to the window to have one last look at the stars shining over the tops of the mountains.

The earth and all its problems were very far away.

Here in this enchanted world they were halfway to Heaven and Heaven was within sight.

She put out the lights except one that was by her bed.

It was hidden behind the muslin curtains which fell from a golden corona above it.

She felt as if the minutes were ticking very slowly by until the door opened.

The Major came in, and when he reached the bed, he stood looking down at her.

Her fair hair was falling over her shoulders, and he could see the outline of her breasts through the thin silk of her nightgown.

He stood looking at her.

Then, throwing the robe he was wearing onto a chair, he got into bed beside her.

He was about to take her in his arms, when Mavina put up her hand as if to stop him.

"I have . . . something to . . . tell you," she said.

The Major was very still.

He thought that confessions would spoil what was for him the most perfect moment in his life.

He wanted to tell her to keep it, whatever it was, to herself.

But the words would not come.

Then in a little voice that he could hardly hear, Mavina said:

"Mama did not . . . tell me what . . . happens when people . . . make love. If I do . . . anything . . . wrong . . . please tell me and . . . do not be . . . cross. I want to . . . love you as . . . you want . . . to be . . . loved."

The Major shut his eyes.

This was what he wanted, yet what he was sure he would never find, and why he had determined never to marry.

Very gently he put his arms round Mavina.

"My Darling, my Sweet," he said, "my innocent little wife. There is nothing you could do that would be wrong as long as you love me."

"I love . . . you . . . you know . . . I love . . . you," Mavina cried. "I love . . . you with my . . . heart and my . . . soul. When I thought you were . . . sending me back . . . to England I . . . wanted to . . . die."

The Major drew her closer.

"You will not die," he said, "but live with me and

we will be so happy that the whole world will envy us."

He pulled her a little closer still.

Then he was kissing her forehead, her eyes, her straight little nose, her lips, and the softness of her neck.

The ecstasy she had felt before swept through Mavina, but it was even more vivid, more intense.

As he went on kissing her, she could feel his heart beating frantically against her heart.

She felt it was impossible to feel such ecstasy and still be on earth.

"I love . . . you . . . I love . . . you," she wanted to say, but she knew her whole body was saying it for her.

With every breath she drew she loved her Husband more.

She had no idea how strictly the Major was controlling himself so that he would not frighten or hurt her.

At the same time, he knew that the icicle, as Lady Flora had called him, had melted at last.

His whole body was burning, not just with passion but with something far more spiritual.

It was the spirit of life moving through him and reaching out to Mavina.

He was aware that just as the flames of life were rising in him, they were flickering in her.

He kissed and touched her until she moved against him and he knew they were already a part of each other.

This was the moment when he would make her his completely and absolutely.

As he did so, they were swept up into the sky.

The light which had blessed them when they were married enveloped them.

They became part of the stars and held the moon in their arms.

They were together in a Heaven of love.

The love which comes from God.

A little while later Mavina kissed her Husband's shoulders.

His arms tightened round her.

"Are you all right, my Darling?" he asked.

"So happy ... so very ... very ... happy," Mavina murmured.

Then she said in a soft voice:

"I did not ... know ... love was so ... wonderful ... so marvellous."

"That is what I wanted you to feel," the Major replied.

"I did ... but ..."

"But what?" he asked.

There was a pause, then Mavina asked:

"Does it ... only ... happen ... once?"

There was an expression in the Major's eyes which no woman had ever seen before.

"It happens, my precious, perfect, little wife," he replied, "whenever you love me."

"Oh ..."

There was a lilting joy in the sound.

Then Mavina said, her words falling over and over: "I love ... you ... I love ... you, my marvellous charming, handsome Husband. Love me ... please love me ... please ..."

ABOUT THE AUTHOR

Barbara Cartland, the world's most famous romantic novelist, who is also a historian, playwright, lecturer, political speaker and television personality, has now written 622 books and sold over six hundred and twenty million copies all over the world.

She has also had many historical works published and has written four autobiographies as well as the biographies of her mother and that of her brother, Ronald Cartland, who was the first Member of Parliament to be killed in the last war. This book has a preface by Sir Winston Churchill and has been republished with an introduction by Sir Arthur Bryant.

Love at the Helm, a novel written with the help and inspiration of the late Earl Mountbatten of Burma, Great Uncle of His Royal Highness, The

Prince of Wales, is being sold for the Mountbatten Memorial Trust.

She has broken the world record for the last twenty-one years by writing an average of twenty-three books a year. In the *Guinness Book of World Records* she is listed as the world's top-selling author.

Miss Cartland in 1987 sang an Album of Love Songs with the Royal Philharmonic Orchestra.

In private life Barbara Cartland, who is a Dame of the Order of St. John of Jerusalem and Chairman of the St. John Council in Hertfordshire, has fought for better conditions and salaries for Midwives and Nurses.

She championed the cause for the Elderly in 1956, invoking a Government Enquiry into the "Housing Condition of Old People."

In 1962 she had the Law of England changed so that Local Authorities had to provide camps for their own Gypsies. This has meant that since then thousands and thousands of Gypsy children have been able to go to School, which they had never been able to do in the past, as their caravans were moved every twenty-four hours by the Police.

There are now fifteen camps in Hertfordshire and Barbara Cartland has her own Romany Gypsy Camp called "Barbaraville" by the Gypsies.

Her designs "Decorating with Love" are being sold all over the U.S.A. and the National Home Fashions League made her, in 1981, "Woman of Achievement."

She is unique in that she was one and two in the Dalton list of Best Sellers, and one week had four books in the top twenty.

Barbara Cartland's book *Getting Older, Growing*

Younger has been published in Great Britain and the U.S.A. and her fifth cookery book, *The Romance of Food*, is now being used by the House of Commons.

In 1984 she received at Kennedy Airport America's Bishop Wright Air Industry Award for her contribution to the development of aviation. In 1931 she and two R.A.F. Officers thought of, and carried, the first aeroplane-towed glider airmail.

During the War she was Chief Lady Welfare Officer in Bedfordshire, looking after 20,000 Servicemen and women. She thought of having a pool of Wedding Dresses at the War Office so a Service Bride could hire a gown for the day.

She bought 1,000 gowns without coupons for the A.T.S., the W.A.A.F.s and the W.R.E.N.S. In 1945 Barbara Cartland received the Certificate of Merit from Eastern Command.

In 1964 Barbara Cartland founded the National Association for Health of which she is the President, as a front for all the Health Stores and for any product made as alternative medicine.

This is now a £65 million turnover a year, with one-third going in export.

In January 1968 she received *La Médeille de Vermeil de la Ville de Paris*. This is the highest award to be given in France by the City of Paris. She has sold 30 million books in France.

In March 1988 Barbara Cartland was asked by the Indian Government to open their Health Resort outside Delhi. This is almost the largest Health Resort in the world.

Barbara Cartland was received with great enthusiasm by her fans, who feted her at a reception in the City, and she received the gift of an embossed plate from the Government.

Barbara Cartland was made a Dame of the Order of the British Empire in the 1991 New Year's Honours List by Her Majesty, The Queen, for her contribution to Literature and also for her years of work for the community.

Dame Barbara has now written 622 books, the greatest number by a British author, passing the 564 books written by John Creasey.

AWARDS

1945 Received Certificate of Merit, Eastern Command, for being Welfare Officer to 5,000 troops in Bedfordshire.

1953 Made a Commander of the Order of St. John of Jerusalem. Invested by H.R.H. The Duke of Gloucester at Buckingham Palace.

1972 Invested as Dame of Grace of the Order of St. John in London by The Lord Prior, Lord Cacia.

1981 Received "Achiever of the Year" from the National Home Furnishing Association in Colorado Springs, U.S.A., for her designs for wallpaper and fabrics.

1984 Received Bishop Wright Air Industry Award at Kennedy Airport, for inventing the aeroplane-towed Glider.

1988 Received from Monsieur Chirac, The Prime Minister, The Gold Medal of the City of Paris, at the Hotel de la Ville, Paris, for selling 25 million books and giving a lot of employment.

1991 Invested as Dame of the Order of The British Empire, by H.M. The Queen at Buckingham Palace for her contribution to Literature.